John Lear served in Germany in the early days of the Allied Occupation, and in Austria; he studied German and Russian at Cambridge, and for some years trained interpreters. He is married, has two sons, two daughters and a Labrador, and teaches in Hampshire.

John Lear

# Death In Leningrad

Pluto Press

First published in 1986 by Pluto Press Limited,
The Works, 105a Torriano Avenue, London NW5 2RX
and Pluto Press Australia Limited, PO Box 199, Leichhardt,
New South Wales 2040, Australia. Also Pluto Press,
27 South Main Street, Wolfeboro, New Hampshire 03894-2069

7 6 5 4 3 2 1

90 89 88 87 86

Set by Sunrise Setting, Torquay, Devon
Printed in Great Britain by Cox & Wyman Ltd,
Reading, Berks

British Library Cataloguing in Publication Data

Lear, John
   Death in Leningrad.—(Pluto crime)
   I. Title
823'.914[F]      PR6062.E2/

ISBN 0 7453 0142 8 (pbk)
      0 7453 0135 5 (hbk)

And you all know security
Is mortals' chiefest enemy.

Shakespeare, *Macbeth*

Our separation is an illusion:
I am inseparable from you,
my shadow is upon your walls,
my reflection is in your canals,
my steps sound in the Hermitage halls
and on the resounding bridges . . .

Akhmatova, *Poem without a Hero*

# 1.

It was hot in Leningrad that August. The vast expanse of blue above the glinting gold of domes, cupolas and spires was dotted with fluffy white good-weather clouds. Baroque façades shone out in every shade of azure, turquoise, ochre and peach. Waterways shimmered against their glittering walls of reddish granite and the dark undersides of the countless bridges. Dusty pigeons got in and out of the way of workers heading, in this part of the city, for offices and shops. Of the workers, a few were stocky or dumpy enough to meet the western preconception of the typical Russian, but a surprising number were slim, straight-backed girls and women in bright summer frocks.

Ashweald held first one, then another narrow door-flap open to let the hostel cat go first. Once outside in the sun, she paused to stretch a leg very slowly. Awkwardly placed in the air-lock-like entrance, he waited for her to stretch the other leg and proceed, but in the manner of cats everywhere, she did neither, so that he had to step over her in order to set off up the street. A little way ahead, a buff-coloured *Zhiguli* swung into the kerb. The driver detached wiper-blades and wing-mirror and locked them in the boot before darting up the office steps.

At the junction with Dzerzhinsky Street, he started to cross, not seeing the light was at red, and as he did so a black *Volga* came bouncing over the hump of Stone Bridge and charged him like a bull. He leapt back. The buffet of air reeked of superheated metal, oil and rubber. Bloody maniac!

1

The sheer width, straightness and emptiness of the streets fired a kind of madness in drivers! *Drivers prone to madness –* just the sort of note for the travel diary he didn't keep. And then the women, the slim straight-backed women in their bright summer frocks . . . Against the light, and light was everywhere, not wearing a slip produced a shock effect to rival that of the driving.

A sudden whiff of age-old urine spiced with some appalling disinfectant made it impossible to breathe for quite some distance. *The summer stink known to every St Petersburger who cannot rent a* dacha *for the summer* . . . Not so very much had changed since that July *of terrible heat*, a hundred and twenty years ago now, when Raskolnikov set out to borrow money from the moneylender woman, and came away with just one rouble fifteen. But on this August morning of considerable heat Ashweald's thoughts were more of Warburton. Of Warburton wringing beer from his Squadron-Leaderly moustaches with a leisurely deliberation eloquent of Squadron-Leaderly wisdom, experience, gen of the pukka sort, although in National Service he had stuck at Pilot Officer.

'You mean, old boy, you really don't know *why* they never let us visit the Union?'

Knowing that whatever he said would serve as a cue, Ashweald had murmured something about security.

'Security, old scout, is just the smoke-screen, the camouflage netting . . . The common-or-garden high-octane truth, old scout, is that our lords and masters – on whom be peace! – require, nay, stipulate that as few as humanly possible shall get within a whisker's width of one very basic fact. Namely, that a nation that can't produce enough bog-paper for its needs, let along get a bog to flush, presents a threat to nobody and nothing – except its own public health . . .'

Wasn't that oversimplifying a bit – like Hitler saying you had only to give the Russian door a kick to bring down the whole rotten shack?

'Not talking about kicking doors, laddie.' Stifled belch. 'The subject is bogs, Soviets for the use of, which don't, I gather, ever have doors . . . No, dear boy, the very orange pip – ' Comma-length pause to down the Strong Old Special and towel the moustaches like dripping dogs – 'the very orange pip of my contention is that our Int. effort v. the Union, the whole costly catastrophe, is a self-perpetuating, king-sized con-trick which, for the sake of our overdrafts – God bless 'em and all who sail in 'em – we must pray will continue to flourish.'

'Fancy the other half?'

'I would, squire, if you insist.'

'Jo, two more when you're ready. SO Special. Pints.'

'No, believe you me, old son, if only one quarter's true of what they say who have been and seen – not FO smart-pants, Socialist MPs or Trade Unionists who don't know a corkscrew from a cranking-handle, but ale-drinking hardheads like you or me – then this pathetic little island remnant of Greatness-now-defunct has nothing whatsoever to fear from the Union. What it *has* got to fear is that *our* Olde-Time antics may one day bust the bank. No. No doubt about it. Wrong side of the hangar door, laddie, that's us. Shut in for the duration by a door of unknowing. Terrible thing!'

But the door of the *Visla* snack bar was open. A strawy, cabbagey odour advertised that from a little way off. Ashweald descended the few steps and made the long walk to the far counter where there was no queue. The buxom blonde assistant gave him smiling attention.

'Good morning. A full one?'

'A full one, please.'

She worked the coffee dispenser. 'What else?'

'Soured cream. Two eggs. Bread, two slices.' The display was meagre. 'Any butter?'

'Not at the given moment.'

'Tomato salad, please. That's all.'

3

Abacus beads clicked. 'Eighty-five kopeks.' She counted out change. 'I wish you health.'

He had the feeling that this, his third visit, established him as a regular, as someone who didn't stand out as foreign, and was well pleased. He took a fork and spoon: there were never any knives, which, on butter days, must make spreading difficult, since the spoons and forks bent like rubber. There were never any trays, either, and so he assembled his purchases on a corner of the counter and cast around for somewhere to sit.

'Here, Nick.' It was Carvel, leader of the small party of Russianists of which Ashweald was a member. Carvel had the room next to his at the hostel and shared the tiny bathroom of primitive character and uncertain plumbing. He bore an incongruous – and possibly cultivated – resemblance to the First Folio portrait of William Shakespeare, there being no point at which lofty brow seemed to end and dome of head to begin. At Heathrow, Ashweald had warmed to him the moment they met. His shepherding of the party was as unobtrusive and effective as his firmness in face of difficulty.

'How was the river?' he asked.

'Marvellous.'

'Riot of vistas, panoramas, buildings, reflections, wheeling gulls? Brilliant sky, not-so-brilliant loudspeaker commentary, lee-side pong of lav.?'

'Astonishing, Holmes. You might have been there.'

'Elementary, Watson, I *have* been – often.' He grinned his peculiar grin, a brightening of the eyes that rippled over temples and forehead like sunlight on water. 'Well, may your evening on the Neva succour and comfort you throughout the double-dose of Chichibayev beginning' – he consulted his watch – 'in forty-five minutes from now.'

'You make him sound grim.'

'Say that he shares with tripe and onions the distinction of being not everyone's favourite dish.'

'And not much scope for cutting.'

4

'Not with our numbers. Illness is a sufficient cause, but pleaded too often could put you into a local hospital, which I don't recommend. The best thing's to say you've a *consultation*, which means you've an appointment to see some local specialist in your line of country.'

'So it's grin and bear it?'

''Fraid so. Remembering always to show due deference to Chichibayev. He's Course Organizer. The Cultural Agreement lays down that there shall be so many hours' instruction, and Comrade Chichibayev is there to keep count. And that reminds me . . .' With a *You permit?* to his Russian neighbour he reached across to the tumbler in the centre of the table, extracted one of the small rectangles of paper supplied for holding sausages – when available – or wiping spoons, wrote a few words and slipped the paper into his spectacles case. 'Had a telegram via the Embassy. We've got a late addition to the course. Arriving this evening. Which means I've got to remember: one, to tell Chichibayev, and two, to meet the plane at Pulkovo.'

'Mind if I tag along for interest?'

'Be delighted. Help carry the bags.'

They walked back to the hostel together. Reflected in the window of a *gastronom* displaying a dozen or so drab brown-paper bags containing, Carvel hazarded, pale, fragile eggs or disagreeable sausage, they made an odd pair: Ashweald, tall, greying and military; Carvel, short, bald, bearded and donnish. By way of a change they continued on over Stone Bridge and turned left along the Griboyedov Canal. At this early hour no one was fishing. No lovers leant over the railings. The only obstacles were emaciated pigeons.

Walking in silence, at ease in each other's company, they soon came to the Bank Footbridge, a narrow, delicate structure supported by parallel cables issuing at either end from the jaws of black, gold-pinioned griffons sejant. Ashweald slapped one on the rump with a murmured *Good*

5

*boy* as he passed.

'From which, Watson,' Carvel said dramatically, 'I infer the dog-man, rather than the cat-man. And the dog, I'd be prepared to wager, is a keen, lean Labrador, *not* what my tweedy aunt would call a Slobrador.'

'Remarkable!'

'Walks to school with you each day, and lies, good as gold, at your feet while you teach?'

'Comes to school at night when I do a final round. By day he guards the home.'

'*Final round?* Night patrol? At a prestigious place like yours? By a senior member of staff? You do surprise me.'

'It's something I took on – *just to help out* – when the Head Porter died, then got stuck with when his replacement flatly refused to work unsocial hours.'

'*You* work unsocial hours but not the porter . . .'

'Staff exploitation – life's blood of the system. Without it there's not a public school in the country that wouldn't fold.'

'Like to hear you in play with old Ernie. He's our ravening Socialist. Teaches in a bloody great comprehensive in some bloody awful conurbation. Still, I'm sure your nightly walk has its compensations. Good for the heart and so on. I say, just look at that!'

He looked with Carvel along the canal to the green and white whirls of the onion domes of the Church of the Saviour on the Blood, but with no pleasure or quickening of pulse. Without knowing, Carvel, in the manner of a merciless analyst, had shocked him into recalling an incident he had done his best to shut out and forget because it made such a mockery of the present. What Ashweald saw was not the canal but the tree-arched path to school, black and white under the moon. He saw Rob standing and growling, and felt again the jerk of alarm as a figure stepped purposefully from the shadows.

Archie! Bloody Archie! Archie whom Ashweald had himself

recruited for the Old Firm out of friendship and kindness of heart! Archie, who years after Ashweald and Sue had resigned from the Firm, had come for a weekend, giving out, not entirely convincingly, that he too had resigned and was now in other employment, after which he'd dropped neither card at Christmas nor line in between, for fifteen years!

Archie, who had come, checked up on their loyalty, then lain low, as if their friendship had never been, now stepped genially from the shadows as if they'd parted only yesterday, as if their friendship, begun at Cambridge, had endured without a break . . .

'I've not been straight, Nick,' he confessed. 'I'm sorry . . .' But who in the Firm ever *was* straight? Why should he expect to pass as straight now? Why not phone? Why come popping out of the darkness like the Erl-king? After fifteen bloody years!

'Listen, Nick . . . Listen, *please*. When you and Sue married, when you and Sue got out, it seemed right and proper to distance ourselves. You must see that. Otherwise, Christ, you know the form: where two or more Firm-types are gathered together, there shall the Firm be sole topic of conversation . . . We'd have gone on talking shop as if you were still on the inside. You know we would. Quite apart from which, the odd doubt did raise its ugly head, as you must have suspected. The letters you and Sue wrote on behalf of our tricky friend Peter . . . Your birthday and Christmas cards to Peter in prison . . . Rumours about your having quit on *moral grounds* . . . OK. When I came, I came, amongst other things, to establish whether you and Sue were the same loyal citizens you'd always been. I let myself be sent. I ought not to have. I ought instead to have sprung to attention, saluted the shit-bucket, fired off the Forster dictum about betraying a friend, chancing they wouldn't twig what a bloody silly hypothesis that is and be shamed into silence . . .'

So Ashweald took Archie to his study in the school and there, in the light, saw that Archie's eyes still flashed mad and

7

unusually large behind their thick lenses, and that Archie's suit was still off the peg, and still not the right one.

'I'm listening, Archie, say your piece. It's hellish late and I've still got marking to do.'

'All right, no beating about the bush. I'd like you to go where you were always told you mustn't. Soviet Union. Leningrad. Month of August. Advanced course for Russianists. Attend classes. Cultivate the social side. Just that.'

Oh, the warm glow, the sense of pride, the satisfaction at feeling *wanted*, at being recognized as the man for the job! Nothing, nothing under the sun so dulling to the critical faculty as that particular warm glow, that particular sense of pride, that particular satisfaction!

'Why *me*? Why, after so many years, *me*?'

'You fit the bill. Bona fide teacher. Impeccable standing . . . You know us, our interests and so on, but on the face of it you're quite unconnected with us. You speak Russian like a native.'

'*Attend classes? Cultivate the social side?* What the hell will that do to advance the Firm's cause?'

'I honestly can't say . . . I've got a hunch, a vague feeling . . . It's totally imprecise, but it's there. It's there. Something like when you're driving – that urge to brake – you've no notion why, you can see nothing to justify it, but you *do* brake. The next instant you see the hazard, and you thank God for that uncanny urge to brake early and for no apparent reason. Well, my uncanny urge now is to send you, to have you there – where I can't go – to have you there on my behalf . . . Try to see it like one of those Christies where Poirot just happens to be of the party. There's a certain something which he senses. Or there's no certain anything. But when the balloon goes up, Poirot's there to note colour, size, direction of flight . . . I'd like you to do just that . . .'

'Too eloquent, too seductively persuasive, Archie – I'm

too old a trout for that moth-eaten fly!'

Archie shook his head uncomprehendingly, pushed his spectacles more firmly onto the bridge of his nose with a middle finger, stared intently at the floor as if reading some message in the pattern of the carpet. 'Forty years of Russian, Nick, and never a glimpse of Russia – I'd have thought this was a chance to grab with both hands. I know I'd grab it. Look, I'm pushing it your way – trying, if you like, to make amends. It could be pure holiday.'

'*Spy who came in from the Cold*, Archie – I expect you've read it. Liz Gold gets given a little foreign holiday, in East Germany. It costs Liz her life.'

'Fiction, Nick. Oversimplified, schoolboy stuff.'

'Like those Christies where Poirot happens to be one of the party.'

Archie returned his gaze to the floor, leaning further over the arm of his chair as if trying to find the right place in his invisible script. 'Let's not bandy words, Nick. I'm not here to play the demonic spy-master. Or pitch you into some life-or-death struggle. I've too much regard for you and Sue. What I've told you is all I've got to tell, and no more and no less than the truth.'

'Take a hell of a lot to half-convince me of that.'

Archie raised his eyes. 'What *will* half-convince you?'

'Oh, go to hell.'

'I'm asking in all seriousness, Nick. I've not come all the way down here and stood cooling my heels for a couple of hours for the fun of it. I'm asking you to name your price.'

'To go to Leningrad for a month and socialize – socialize with who – the natives or our contingent?'

'Bit of both maybe – ear to the ground, and perhaps the odd mike judiciously placed.'

'And if action's called for?'

'You must do what you judge possible.'

'And if I come back empty-handed?'

'Then that's it. Here's the money. Thank you very much.'

He should have stopped the whole thing at the *Go to hell* – not let Archie talk on, not let the spark be fanned into a blaze – a blaze of enthusiasm not only to see Russia, but to be back in the old harness, pulling the old cart along the old devious ruts . . . If Sue had been there he'd have choked Archie off, and that would have been that. No. If Sue had been there, Archie would never have made such an offer. It had not been just for the sake of security that Archie had lain in wait to catch him on his own.

'I'd need some sort of assurance against not coming back,' he heard himself saying. 'A hefty sum – a hundred and fifty thousand, say, lodged in a deposit account in my name. The relevant documents to be lodged by me in a sealed envelope with my solicitor. Instructions for disposal to be made by me. If I die the whole lot goes to my estate. Otherwise I get fifteen thousand a year, or part of a year, served in prison. If all goes well – '

'Which it will.'

'If all goes well I return the hundred and fifty thousand, less my honorarium.'

'Of what? Shall we say, five thousand?'

Ashweald thought of his children's small but persistent credit-card debts, thought how he would like to make up to them for years of hitch-hiking, of doing without books, clothes, food. 'I'd rather we said ten.'

Archie, to his surprise, assented. 'Ten, then – in consideration of your willingness to emerge from mothballs. You *are*, I take it, willing – for ten thousand pounds?' He reached into an inner pocket and produced not a hundred and fifty thousand in notes of large denomination, which would have accorded with Ashweald's rocketing sense of unreality, but an application form which he proffered with the furtive confidence of an insurance broker. 'To apply for the course on,' he said. 'You've got about five weeks to bring Sue round to the idea – of going on the course, I mean. The other is strictly between ourselves.'

'What if they don't accept me?'

'It must have escaped your notice that Russian studies in this country are in their death agony. We lash out on weaponry, cut back on linguists. There'll be fewer applicants than vacancies.'

'And I come to you for briefing?'

'No, you do not. I've told you all there is. You stay absolutely severed from the Firm – that's why I've come like this – I hope, inconspicuously. Also you must not, in any circumstances, identify yourself as Firm. *That* is absolutely essential.'

'You said something about a mike.'

'*Hearing aids* we call them now. I'll send the box of tricks to you at the school, parcelled as language lab equipment. Looks like a small portable transistor receiver-cum-cassette-recorder but enables you to receive, monitor and record a couple of radio mikes. Test it, get the hang of it before you go. Vast improvement on what we used to have. Customs-proof, too.'

'How do I communicate with you?'

'You don't. Our Russia map, as you may remember, has as many blanks as Africa before Livingstone. It'll be a question of soldiering on for the whole month on your Jack Jones.'

'No embassy contact?'

'Not at any price!'

Out of one jacket pocket Archie tugged a cherry-wood pipe and out of the other a green-and-cream tin of Exmoor Hunt Mixture. 'Do you mind?'

'No,' Ashweald said, but secretly he minded very much. It was the tobacco he himself had smoked in his smoking days.

'I want you there on *my* behalf, as I've said, as *my* observer . . . ' The words came out between puffs at the pipe. The match flame reared each time he stopped drawing. 'And I want that fact kept strictly between you and me . . . Which it couldn't be if the embassy came into it. I can't put it any more clearly than that.' He waved a hand to disperse the denser areas of smoke. 'I wish I could give you more help, be more precise, say *Watch for a sea-faring man with one leg . . .* '

'Not that it helped Jim Hawkins much, that particular advice.'

'Really? I don't recall. But there is one thing I can, and will, do when the course list gets finalized, and that is send you a second, doctored copy. You remember our special type-face features? OK, get your magnifier out, and any name with a hair-line gap somewhere on the first vowel will be the name of someone worth watching more than the rest.'

'Why?' Ashweald inquired of the aromatic smoke.

'That just brings us back in a circle to my hunch, my vague feeling . . . I really can't say more.'

'Who's Head of Ops now? You?'

'No. Don is. Don Warburton. You're lucky – you only knew him in his pub-bore days. God, you should meet the *club*-bore he is now – goes with having graduated to *Sir* Donald!'


Chichibayev still had a substantial part of his hour to run. After which would come an army-style ten-minute break for a smoke, followed by Chichibayev's second hour. He was speaking with an admirable fluency well adapted to the self-important air of absolute authority favoured by all Europeans save the British.

'. . . A fact is, has always been, and will always remain, a fact, which in itself is a fact of no small importance to the world-outlook characterized as Socialist Realism . . . '

Facts of more immediate concern to Ashweald were Richard Carvel and Eleanor Archer-Smythe, both marked out by Archie in the course list as specially worthy of attention, and both this morning sitting side by side. The seat nearest the door was favoured by Carvel as the best situated from which to make announcements at the end of lectures. But this morning he had moved along, vacating it for Eleanor, who had arrived ten minutes late. Her entry caused

Chichibayev to break off and strike the pose of the Great Soloist bearing with an accompanist who cannot find the key of the piano. Into the awful silence and Chichibayev's withering stare Eleanor had breathed an ill-pronounced *izvinite!*, at which Chichibayev had disburdened himself of an ironical *pozhaluysta* before resuming.

Despite the bright sun, Eleanor was still wearing an impeccably cut Burberry, and, clapped on a torrent of grey hair, a broad-brimmed felt hat. In common with the other six ladies of the party, she was writing busily, either recording every slowly-delivered word, or, more likely, keeping up her end of an extensive correspondence. Carvel, eyes fixed on Chichibayev, was a veritable statue of The Bard.

Ashweald gave up trying to follow the argument and concentrated on the beauty of the Russian sounds and the manner of their delivery. Chichibayev looked like the Highgate bust of Marx complete with plinth. His voice was appropriately resonant.

'. . . So now, before we break . . .'

Roused from his open-eyed nap, Ashweald saw that Chichibayev was already half-way to the door.

'. . . are there any questions?'

Chichibayev was already opening the door.

'. . . No? . . .'

Chichibayev was gone.

At the end of the corridor, commanding the entrances to the lavatories, stood a table bearing a number of large empty cans usable as ashtrays. Here, in the breaks, the smokers gathered, East Germans, Hungarians, Czechs and Austrians attending similar but separate courses, and the few smokers of the British party. They formed an unyielding, somewhat sullen throng, and considerable force and perseverance were required of any who would win through to the lavatory. But win through Ashweald did, and there he encountered Ernie Oldroyd, curiously crouched so as to avoid contact with the seatless pan and dolefully considering a fistful of fivers.

'No, Ernie, don't – relief is at hand. I've an old *Literaturnaya Gazeta* in my briefcase. I'll fetch it.'

'You're a gradely lad, Nick, for all your posh talk.'

'Cost you a fiver though.'

'Away to buggery!'

Ernie was doyen of the party. He had been ten times to the Soviet Union and completed several Russian courses without, as he put it, ever really getting on top of all the letters of the alphabet. Nevertheless, whether in Moscow or Leningrad – or, for all Ashweald knew, Ulan Bator – he disposed of a seemingly inexhaustible list of Russian girl-friends, any of whom, phoned by a Russian speaker on Ernie's behalf, would arrive bearing gifts and sweep Ernie off to improbable restaurants with bands and dancing and bills with near-three-digit totals. At Heathrow he had been seen off by a formidable, stylishly tweedy lady, every inch the family-planner, marriage-guider and meals-on-wheelser rolled into one. At the airport in Moscow, to the general amusement, he had been subjected to the humiliation of having several of a stock of different-coloured condoms unrolled and held up for inspection by customs officials.

'Not one bloody word did I get of the first half and not one bloody word will I get of the second,' Ernie announced as Ashweald delivered *Literaturnaya Gazeta*. 'Wish I were a clever bugger like yourself.'

'Not to worry. You're not missing a great deal.'

'Like to judge for myself though. I came to see the good in the country, not pick bloody fault.'

'Any more of your ingratitude and I snatch my paper back and leave you to your fifty quid's worth.'

'Reckon you would and all. Still, I'll save *your* life one day – make us quits . . .'

'Oh dear, Nick, not suffering, I hope?' Eleanor asked, exhaling the dense blue smoke of a cheroot. '*Twice in five minutes*. One can't help noticing. You're welcome, you know, to some of my little green pills.'

'Very kind, Eleanor, but the sufferer's Ernie. I'm just lending material support.'

'Then I'm glad – the ungrateful man. I offered *him* some of my little green pills, and do you know what he said? *It's a local trouble, lass, so there'll be a local jollop for it*. And off he goes to that sinister little *apteka* by Stone Bridge and eventually comes back with the biggest bottle of the horridest colour ever. God knows how he managed it with his non-existent Russian . . .'

The lunch break was from twelve until twelve forty-five, time enough for most to grab a bite at the Institute cafeteria. Ashweald waited until he saw that both Eleanor and her room-neighbour Helen were of the queue, then returned to the hostel where he extracted their key from the drawer together with his own. The chambermaids were at lunch and the corridor was empty as he let himself into Eleanor and Helen's set.

Since last evening, when he had drunk a nightcap with Eleanor in her room, a clothes' line had been stretched in the short entrance hall. Set against the prim exterior of Helen Blore, the stylish black underwear pegged to it surprised him.

In Eleanor's room Ashweald checked that the radio microphone he had attached to the underside of the massive wardrobe, was still in position. He then switched the wall loudspeaker to one of the channels it relayed from a central receiver. Massed balalaikas were twanging out *The crescent moon is shining* . . . Lifting the loudspeaker from its mounting, he saw that what he conceived to be the bugging microphone had not been tampered with. Replacing the loudspeaker, he turned it off, and stepped boldly into the still empty corridor.

Examining the wall loudspeaker in Carvel's room, he found that a terminal on which one lead of the supposed bugging mike relied, had been loosened just enough for it to become detached. And that, he mused, lunching off processed cheese, black bread and a tomato the size of a cooking apple, seemed to mark Carvel out as an amateur, but as an amateur taking precautions against being bugged. The professional would ask *why* a mike should be positioned where it could do no good when the loudspeaker was playing; and would conclude that it might well be a blind intended to encourage the suspicious victim to unplug the speaker and expose himself, without the cover of radio noise, to the attentions of other, better concealed microphones. Accordingly, Ashweald deemed Carvel to be a point up on Eleanor, and when he had finished lunch and several cans of Lager, the product of foreign-currency shopping under Carvel's tutelage, he attached his remaining radio microphone to the back of Carvel's wardrobe.

# 2.

Pulkovo was a film-set airport waiting for actors, extras and technicians to walk on and bring it to life, and the effect was restful. A beer, a glass of wine, a cup of coffee would have lent the restfulness a certain piquancy, but they were not to be had.

'You watch Gate 1, I'll cover Gate 2,' Carvel proposed, when arrival indicator, telephone information and loudspeaker announcement contradicted each other. Reacting as westerners and reluctant to believe that they could be so comprehensively misinformed, they decided they must themselves be at fault. They were not yet acclimatized, had not yet accustomed themselves to endure total uncertainty with absolute resignation.

'Mason's the name,' Carvel called over the widening distance. '*Irina* Mason . . . Miss . . . '

At his gate Ashweald could see only a militiaman speaking inaudibly and incessantly into a telephone attached to the wall against which he was leaning comfortably, contriving to look at nothing in particular. Then, just as Ashweald was on the point of concluding that he must be at the wrong gate at the wrong time on the wrong day, a trickle of people emerged from somewhere and came towards the gate, a trickle that soon swelled into a stream. The militiaman took no notice but went on talking into his telephone, with the air of one who has learnt *War and Peace* by heart and means to prove it.

That was her. It must be. Costume, stockings, shoes, set her apart. The peaches-and-cream complexion – a phrase of

Sue's that had never before seemed so apt – showed her plainly to be British. He stepped forward. 'Irina Mason?'

The open, cheerful look turned into puzzlement. No, she said, with the emphatic clarity of a BBC Russian lesson, she was Mariya – Mariya Vassilkova.

Ashweald asked to be forgiven and the plainly-British Russian went her way with a *pozhaluysta* as pert as Chichibayev's to Eleanor had been ironic.

'Forgive me,' the Russian voice contained a tremble of merriment, 'but I couldn't help overhearing . . . '

Turning, he became aware of a Slavonic young lady with high cheekbones and raven hair swept back into a bun.

'*Irina Mason – eto ya.*'

Gravely, for all the world like natives of the country, they shook hands. 'I'm Nick Ashweald. Let me take your cases.'

'How very kind of you to meet me,' Irina said in English.

Carvel, when they joined him, insisted on relieving Ashweald of a case, disregarding his protests about balance. Outside, on the pavement, they pushed through the queues for express and other buses to the city, and crossed to the car park. Irina's Russianness plainly had its limits, for against the glare of the setting sun, she remained clothed and mysterious beneath her full-skirted summer frock.

Coming, they'd taken the metro to Moskovskaya, and from there a taxi which Carvel, knowing the form, had retained for the return. The car park was practically empty, and the taxi driver, spotting them, came sprinting over and insisted on taking the cases. He was not a tall man, but the progress he made with them, if slow, was cheerful. Slow progress was made also with starting. Whinny succeeded whinny, reminding Ashweald unpleasantly of his own car at home. Now, with no more school fees to pay and the prospect of Archie's ten thousand, he could, in theory, afford something a little less unserviceably second hand . . .

But now they were moving, moving fast, their driver intent on testing steering and suspension to destruction on a surface

18

that might have been purpose built.

Carvel, sitting in front, turned to shout above the din that the vast greenhouses they were now passing, were probably where the outsize tomatoes were grown. A little later he shouted that he would attend to the check-in formalities at the hostel and see Irina settled in her room, but that then, he was afraid, he would have to dash off.

'What's the bath situation?' she asked.

'One to every two-room set. You'll need your own plug.'

'Luxury! I've *got* my own plug.'

'Hot water often between eight and nine, which we may just catch,' Carvel bawled, wincing as metal ground with more than usual violence against metal somewhere beneath the car.

'Would you like to come for a bite to eat afterwards?' Ashweald asked, seizing the opportunity.

In the fraction of time that elapsed before her answer, he expected her to say no, she was too tired. And if she did, he decided, it would be a judgement on him, an admonition to stick to duty, find out where Carvel was going . . .

'How kind. I'd like that.'

Her eyes were a curious grey flecked with blue.


By means of an ear-phone plugged into his innocent-looking transistor, Ashweald checked what, if anything, was being said in Carvel's room.

Helen Blore and Hilda Nettleton – the suppressed Midlands accents were unmistakable – were proposing to spend Saturday and Sunday nights with Russian boy friends, and putting Carvel into the picture, unofficially, since, as they knew and as Carvel reminded them, the arrangement was highly *nedopustimo* – inadmissible.

He switched off. Nothing there worth risking interception for. But the recital of names, addresses, attitudes made painful listening. How could an old Russia-hand like Carvel be so naive as to think his room secure from bugging on the strength of disconnecting that single lead? And how could he, whether he had disconnected it or not, be so very foolish as to let the girls provide material for files on themselves and their Russian friends?

He switched to Eleanor's microphone. No joy.

The long corridor onto which their rooms opened, led, like the extended shaft of a capital T, to a common-room-like area representing the cross-piece, where comfortable chairs and settees stood, together with occasional tables bearing giant cut-glass ashtrays. The left-hand arm terminated in a television set in a neo-baroque cabinet; the right-hand arm, in double glass doors giving onto a landing and the main staircase. Ashweald perched himself on the settee that faced back down the corridor.

Grouped in front of the tele were Ernie, Eleanor and the two rosy-cheeked, blue-chinned young men pigeonholed in Ashweald's mind as schoolmasters. Having his Ancient Mariner's will of this handful of viewers was a venerable trade unionist. His tale was of a year's typical union activity, and the signs were that a year might go into the telling. Eleanor, still in Burberry, was smoking a cheroot with the same aggressive purposelessness that some people put into jogging. The schoolmasters had pencils and notebooks. Ernie, like a spectator of slow-motion tennis, kept switching his head to and fro, looking now at the screen, now at a dictionary on the table beside him, trying to make sense of a slogan behind the speaker, which read:

*Trade unions, being a school for communism in general, must be a school for socialist industrial management in particular . . .*

*Lenin*

Spotting Ashweald, Eleanor heaved herself to her feet and came over. 'Now, young man, are you going to invite me out

20

for dinner?'

'Alas, young lady, I am not.'

There was no earthly reason why not. It was just that something within him jerked stubbornly to a stop, like a cassette at the end of its run. Eleanor was not included on that cassette, and as they talked mock-flippantly of this and that, he prayed that Irina would not come tripping down the corridor to add to the complications of the moment.

'Eleanor, you must excuse me, I've got to go – '

'Go?' The incredulity was monumental, like that of a don denied an essay eight supervisions running. '*Go?* Where?'

'Whither, dear Eleanor, the Tsar himself's obliged to foot it,' he intoned, accelerating rapidly for the glass door.

'Whisky's the thing for Leningrad tum,' she called after him. 'Kills the bug. Come and have some . . . '

He went down a whole flight of the steep stone steps at the rate of one per photographer's second: one, uh, two, uh, three, uh . . . Then he went back up at the same pace. No sign of Eleanor. Whisky's clarion summons having sounded, she had not been slow to obey. The schoolmasters, intent to their very Adam's apples, were still sitting enthralled by Outstanding Ore-Smelter Kravtsov on the rationalization of union business. At the far end of the corridor, Irina was emerging from her room . . .

But now, belatedly, Ashweald remembered that he had not the slightest idea where they could eat, let alone where they were going to. 'We'll try the Nevsky,' he said with a cheerful assurance he certainly did not feel. 'If you're not too tired to walk.'

'Not a bit.'

'How was the bath?'

'Laborious. What *is* the black solid stuff?'

'Rubber pipe? Jointing material? Goodness knows. It looks non-organic.'

'I had the brainwave of filtering the bathwater through the

shower spray. But the spray got choked and shot off the pipe.'

'We've all been caught . . . But be careful . . . ' The pavement was slippery where the aerated-water machines were leaking.

They plunged into the Nevsky and merged with the great river of people flowing both ways at once. The door of the restaurant he had in mind was closed and guarded by a *switzer*. Stretching back from the door, resisting erosion by the general flow were at least a hundred would-be diners. 'So much for the *Kavkazsky*. We'd better take a taxi.'

'Can't we walk? It's such a lovely evening.'

'You really want to? All right. We go over the bridge and turn left.'

'Over People's Bridge and beside the Moyka?'

'So it's not your first visit?'

'It *is* my first visit. I know the area around the hostel from studying the guide book on the plane . . . Oh, but it's the most beautiful little river in the world! *Wistfully beautiful* . . . Those mottled reflections stirring like leaves all the time . . . You hear them in Shostakovich's Fifth . . . ' She fell silent, and when she spoke again her voice was matter of fact. 'I suppose the Cam would look a bit like this, if it weren't for the awful punts and canoes!'

'I can't imagine anything so ghastly shattering the peace and tranquillity of this.'

Irina smiled, an impish, at the same time uncertain and quizzical smile. 'Can't you?'

At that very moment a rakish motor-boat with a sick-sounding engine snarled into sight. In the cockpit a huge red-haired, red-bearded man was lolling, his arms around two girls, holding the wheel steady with a grubby foot. The girls had tightly braided jet-black hair and wore patterned kaftans. All were smoking, languidly.

'Jock with twin sisters Fatima and Jamila,' Ashweald murmured, and Irina laughed. Leaning over the railing they watched the boat until it passed out of sight under People's Bridge.

'There. The wash has stopped splashing. Wistful beauty's restored.'

Here and there, where excavations made it impossible to step off the pavement, they went in single file to make room for people coming the other way. All of them looked admiringly at Irina.

'Wish I wasn't quite so conspicuously foreign,' she said with feeling. 'I seemed to manage not to be when I was a student.'

'Probably because you looked like a student.'

'So why can't I look like a Russian non-student in a summer frock?'

Not knowing her well enough to say, he left it at, 'Your shoulder-bag, your shoes – they're too stylish, too Italian to pass for local products.'

'I hadn't thought of that. With your eye, you should write a column for one of the Sundays – *Ashweald on Soviet Fashion*.'

'And give the world my *one* discovery? That there seem to be as few styles of shoes and handbags as there seem to be types of cars?'

Irina laughed.

He had planned to turn right at Dzerzhinsky Street and make for the *Astoriya* Hotel, where there must surely be a restaurant, but Irina insisted that they turn left onto Red Bridge and then cross the road to look over the other side. There was the *Visla* snack bar, now shut. He was about to say that that was the place for breakfast, but Irina was so plainly lost in thought that he kept silent. Anyway, the problem just then was dinner.

'Sorry, Nick,' her voice came unexpectedly. 'I was miles away. What was it you said?'

A penny for your thoughts, he would have said, again if he had known her better, but just then it occurred to him that a little way up from the *Visla* he'd noticed what looked like a restaurant. 'I think there's a place here that may do,' he said. 'Come on.'

Behind them, at the end of Dzerzhinsky Street, the Admiralty Spire gleamed golden against the paling sky.

There *was* a restaurant, a *Visla* restaurant, companion to the snack bar – the sign hung high above the pavement was of the same design – and they were in luck. The *switzer* let them in without any of the usual officiousness or dourness. The waiter showed them to a candle-lit table of plain unpainted wood. Tall-sided wooden benches created an impression of cosy isolation and intimacy. Ashweald reached for the bulky leather-bound menu with which the waiter had supplied them.

'Ever eaten in this sort of place before?' Irina asked innocently.

He confessed that he had not.

'Would you mind, then, if I ordered?'

He shook his head and held out the menu.

'And not think me over-managing and women's libbish?'

'Of course not.'

'You see, whatever we order from this, they'll write down, slowly and painfully, then half an hour later return and say they haven't got it. Whatever we order, the same thing will happen. In the end we'll be reduced to doing what it's best to do straightaway. 'Comrade waiter!'

'I hear,' the waiter answered and appeared out of the darkness.

'What will you bring us?'

'*Borshch* I will bring, then *shashlyk*, boiled potatoes, cucumber and tomato salad, bread if required, after which peaches and ice-cream.'

'For how much?'

'Ten roubles a head?'

'*A head?*'

'That is, all together.'

'And will there be a dry wine at not more than five roubles? Good. We'd like it now.'

The waiter bowed, thrust the menu under his arm, as a drill sergeant might his pace-stick, and marched off. In less than five minutes he returned with a Georgian wine labelled *dry* but which, on tasting, proved to be medium sweet.

'And nothing drier shall we get, this side of the Bug,' Irina laughed, raising her glass in a mock toast.

'You're clearly no stranger to Russia and its ways.'

'I had a year at Voronezh University as part of the Oxford course, followed by a research term at Moscow.'

'But never came to Leningrad?'

'A scrappy few days wasn't the sort of visit I wanted.'

The waiter, setting down the bowls of *borshch*, looked in surprise hearing their English.

Irina praised the *borshch*, and Ashweald, eating it for the first time, enjoyed it, but whether for its own sake or simply as an adjunct to Irina's company he could not have said. Once or twice as they talked easily of this or that, he thought he sensed a need for sympathy, although not with such certainty as to justify covering her hand with his in the ring of candlelight on the scrubbed table. In any case, he could easily be mistaken. What he took as a need for sympathy might have been no more than nostalgia for David, Bill or Clive far away in UK, although a David, Bill or Clive of her own age who was capable of matching her seriousness and maturity would be an exceptional person indeed. Her very ease in Ashweald's company might betoken an attachment to an older man – a married man perhaps whose wife was blowing the whistle on him . . .

The darkness beyond the table-centred lighting made it impossible to discern the general shape of the room, and it came as a surprise when an accordion-led combo struck up a rumba, and a warm, seductive female voice began to sing:

*Bud' moim zashchitnikom i moyey oporoy . . .*

Couples passed by on their way to dance. He listened to the words:

*Be my guardian spirit, be my sure support,*
*My defending counsel when I appear in court;*
*Be my sound adviser in all and nothing less,*
*Be my one true ally in joy and in distress . . .*

He wished he could hear the second verse, hear the song out, but there was a question to be put, and he felt guiltily that he had already hesitated longer than was mannerly. 'Would you care to dance?'

'Will you feel hurt if I say no? Another time I'd love to.'

At which Ashweald, the non-dancer, breathed a silent prayer of gratitude to the other man, whoever he might be.

They walked back to the hostel by the route Ashweald had followed with Carvel fifteen hours earlier. The air was warm, but now agreeably so; the darkness was only partial. On the bridge of the gold-pinioned griffons they paused to consider the light flickering on the silent black waters, sometimes the perfect image of a globe-shaped lantern, a static full moon, sometimes, at a slight rippling of the surface, a scattered jumble of yellow jig-saw pieces.

The hostel *dezhurnaya* scrutinized them inscrutably. They climbed the stone stairs swiftly and lightly. With increasing clarity they heard the voice of Ernie Oldroyd in full and robust song which, as they arrived on the landing, had reached the refrain:

*Thou hast well drunken, man,*
*who's a fool now?*

A glance through the glass showed most of their compatriots, tooth-glasses in hand, supporting and encouraging

26

Ernie. Eleanor had a bottle in the hand not holding a tooth-glass. Carvel – now Shakespeare unwinding after a successful performance – had Helen Blore on his knee.

'Do we join in?' he asked Irina. 'We'll have to if we go through.'

'Must we? I'd rather not spoil the mood of the evening. But we can't just walk past, can we?'

'We can go on up to the East German floor, walk the length of their corridor and take the far-end stairs down to our own.'

On the East German common-room front, all was quiet. Sleeping figures lay slumped before a television screen of flickering emptiness.

Ashweald waited while Irina tried her door. To their relief, it opened. Solemnly they shook hands and parted.

He tried his own door. That too, mercifully, was unlocked. Then, suddenly, Irina was beside him again.

'I forgot to ask about breakfast.'

'Come and see what you think of the *Visla*?'

'Love to.'

'Meet you at the end of the corridor at 7.45.'

'I'll be there.'

'Good night, Irina.'

'Goodnight, Nicholas.'

Ernie was still at it. The song seemed to have no end:

*Thou hast well drunken, man,*
*who's a fool now?*

# 3.

Eleanor was quick to notice how much Ashweald and Irina enjoyed each other's company, and importuned Ashweald slightly less. Lady Tatiana, who shared a set with Irina, regarded the relationship with amused satisfaction. They breakfasted together, yes, but more often than not in company with Carvel. They sat together at lectures and lessons, and on coaches taking them to places of interest. But Irina, like everyone except Ashweald, knew someone in Leningrad she had to visit. This emerged at their first breakfast together when he suggested a trip on the Neva for that evening. Irina, it turned out, had to ring Valeriya Borisovna – they'd been at Moscow State University together – and Valeriya Borisovna would almost certainly want them to meet straightaway. Could the Neva trip wait until tomorrow? Of course. But he felt stirrings of jealousy, an emotion he had almost forgotten existed.

'I know,' he said in the morning break, 'I can meet you from the metro or the bus-stop when you get back, and see you to the hostel.'

'Terribly sweet. But if I do go, heaven knows when I shall be back. Valya lives a little way out, on the Gulf. Train times will come into it. Besides, I may very well stay the night and catch an early-morning train.'

'Missing breakfast?'

'I honestly can't say.'

'Better put Carvel in the picture.'

'Of course.'

28

*But not in his room for the bugs to pick up*, he wished he could add.

That morning the way to the lavatories lay between the Scylla of Lady Tatiana and the Charybdis of Eleanor, and a navigational error put him at the mercy of Eleanor.

'Nicholas, dear, you're to come to dinner. With some real Russians. This *very* evening. I insist.'

'Love to, but –' But a press of beer paunches, mainly Czech, smothered the rest of the sentence. Silence, he realized, fighting clear, would be taken for assent, but suddenly he didn't care.

'In the foyer, then, at seven. Or better, six-thirty, *chez moi – u menya –* for an aperitif.'

As always, the only other person in the lavatory was Ernie. He was standing one hand on hip, the other on the washbasin, contemplating his massive features in the blotchy mirror.

'Ah, bugger it. Don't know if I want to or if I don't.'

'Hamlet on the battlements.'

'If thou had skits like me, thou'd have nowt to laugh about . . . But I'd a rare old skinful of Scotch last night, and I've a notion it's steadied me.' He peered more closely into the mirror as if to confirm his greater steadiness.

'What's it done to your Russian grammar?'

'Two bloody hours we've just had of passy partiples, all in Russian, and me not sure of the bloody alphabet.'

'Stick it. The march of a thousand miles begins with the very first step.'

'Not if thou'rt marking time!'

Ashweald waved cheerily and re-entered the corridor crush. He meant to return to the classroom and resume his seat beside Irina, but let himself be detained by Lady Tatiana and her reminiscences of Leningrad schooldays.

Eleanor possessed, as well as irritating qualities, the virtue of knowing all there was to know about everyone else on the course, having herself attended the last seven. Everyone, apart from Irina and himself, had at least one previous attendance to their credit, and Ashweald felt sure that curiosity must rank high amongst Eleanor's reasons for cultivating him. So he drank her whisky and awaited interrogation, playing good listener to all that she had to relate.

And so it was that he learnt of the shakiness of Carvel's marriage, Carvel being one of that fashionable and ever-growing band of university teachers who notch up conquests amongst the young ladies who sit at their feet. For Carvel, this month was supposed to provide a much-overdue breathing-space in which to take stock. He learnt that Ernie was AC/DC – half gay, half not – and not to be trusted, and this with some secret amusement, since he had been told by Ernie that Eleanor was lesbian but had still seduced, in long grass at Petrodvoryets, a former pupil of Ashweald's. Lady Tatiana, he learnt further, was the child of a Russian mother and an English father, whose expertise as an engineer, combined with sympathy for the new regime, had led to their setting up home in Leningrad in 1926. They did not return to England until the onset of the purge, by which time Tatiana was through her higher education and about as Russian as you could get. Tatiana's husband was Sir Edward Oakhurst, *the* Sir Edward, the art historian, by virtue of whose contacts Tatiana could fix you a private tour of the Hermitage, which was infinitely preferable to mingling with the mob.

They were half-way down the corridor when Ashweald turned an ankle, still painful and tender from a similar turning a few months before. The rekindled pain made him gasp, and after massaging the place and cursing, he limped to fetch the stick he had brought just in case something of the sort should happen. Eleanor lit a cigarette from the stub of her last, and watched his slow descent of the stairs with concern.

'I'll nip down and phone for a taxi. You can't walk like

that.'

'I can. Otherwise it'll stiffen.'

They cut across the open area of asphalt behind Kazan Cathedral rather than thread through the crowded gardens in front, and joined the Griboyedov Canal Embankment, where they confronted the onion-domed Church of the Saviour on the Blood.

'Tell me,' she paused to cough violently on the smoke of a cigarette pitched an instant before into a two-foot-deep pothole, 'tell me – I'm interested – what exactly does it say to *you*, here and now, that larger-than-life edifice?'

'It looks out of character, out of balance with the plain four-storey buildings lining the canal. Those domes belong on Red Square.'

'True. You know *why* it was built?'

He shook his head.

'Nicholas! And you a Russianist!' The reproach was total.

'I'm keener on literature than history,' he confessed lamely.

'But what the hell's the difference? History, literature – they're one and the same: a conscious shaping of human experience.'

'Except that fiction's not fact.'

'It *can* be, and vice versa.'

'But literature includes poetry – '

'So does history, believe you me. *Tragic* verse, mainly, of beauty and power . . . That church, for instance . . . *Required to prove*: *that* church is both history and a poem . . .

'That church stands where, just over a hundred years ago, Alexander II, after escaping injury from one bomb, walked, literally *walked*, minutes later, straight into another which killed both him and his assassin. The thrower of bomb one, a student, Rysakov – a super-grass he'd be reckoned nowadays – told the police of the other members of the terrorist group. He wanted to save his neck. Who shall blame him? He told of Kibalchich who made the bombs. Of Mikhaylov who was supposed to throw at an earlier point on the route, but funked it, of Emilyanov waiting on a route not followed by the Tsar. He told of Zhelyabov, their leader, already in police hands. And of Zhelyabov's mistress, Sofiya Perovskaya, who masterminded the attack in her lover's absence. All six, super-grass and all, were hanged, publicly and cruelly by a drunken hangman. Sofiya was of good family, petite, blonde, under thirty. There's an artist's impression of the scaffold scene. It's as terrifying as a photograph. Demure little Sofiya wearing her bonnet . . . Sometimes I rehearse what I imagine Sofiya's thoughts were, standing before some pathetic scrap of mirror, donning that pathetic badge of respectability for the very last time.'

On the long escalator, with no advertisements to distract him, he kept seeing, and banishing, the same disagreeable image of a girl, not unlike Irina, in a Salvation-Army bonnet standing bound beside a suspended noose of rope. He concentrated his attention on the uniformed woman seated behind glass far, far below, at the foot of the escalator, talking animatedly into a telephone. What would Sofiya Perovskaya have to say about the new order that had followed the old? Would she be content to don a nondescript uniform and talk endlessly into a phone?

When the train arrived, Eleanor and Ashweald were borne through the gate with the other passengers, as if by a swollen mountain torrent. The few unoccupied seats were grabbed in a twinkling, and Ashweald found himself strap-hanging above a pretty teenage girl. As he tried to see what she was reading, she snapped the book shut, rose with difficulty and motioned him to take her seat. He thanked her, said something about not being so frail as he looked, and remained standing.

'No, you must sit,' the girl said resolutely, and so did the raised eyes of other passengers, amongst whom an old woman muttered something of which he caught only the words *brave man*. So he sat down, and thereafter tried to catch Eleanor's eye with some idea of surrendering the seat to her. But Eleanor, deep in a book, did not look up.

'Military appearance, age, limp, stick – they make you look like a heroic defender of the Motherland. You must accept with good grace,' Eleanor explained afterwards. 'To accept and then pass it on to someone else would be awful ingratitude.'

Outside the metro station a great many flower sellers were holding up their wares and proclaiming their qualities. Eleanor bought yellow roses, Ashweald – marigolds. Their glow matched his feeling at being offered a seat for such a reason. But how galling to know a feeling, and not be worthy of knowing it!

The block in which Eleanor's friends had their flat was modern, tall and ugly. It was one of many, and nothing good could be said of the area except that nature was doing its best to absorb the shock of human intrusion and reassert itself. Grass, shrubs, trees were flourishing. A piece of water shone out healthily amongst them. Ducks could be heard quacking.

The common entrance to the common stairs stank of vomit and worse. *Lift defective* said a grubby card, and as they toiled up flight after flight of stone steps, the smells were reinforced by the reek of stale cabbage.

At last, at a great height, they came to a forbidding Cambridge-oak of a door, and took turns at pressing a bell that produced neither sound nor response. They were turning to go when they heard the sound of an ascending lift. This in itself was astonishing, but far more astonishing was the figure who stepped from the tiny cabin – a Western-glossy-magazine-style of woman in an emerald-green tailored two-piece and with a mane of chestnut hair arranged with a casualness as expensive to achieve as the cut of the two-piece.

'*Vy k Martovym* – Are you for the Martovs?' she asked.

Ashweald broke the silence of awe to say that they were.

'Why not ring?'

'Ringing produces no result.'

'Allow me.'

Her gloved fingers manipulated the bell push as if it were a combination lock, then applied gentle pressure. A bell rang out mightily, and in a few moments, with much drawing of bolts, the oak was thrown open.

Effusive greetings, a cheerful shepherding into a vastly more cheerful world: a well-proportioned, tastefully furnished, book-dominated room, with a view over woodland, a park and a lake to a vast panorama of sunset sky. A choice of wines and *zakuski* was set ready on a fine mahogany table. The yellow roses and fiery marigolds made their entry in suitable bowls.

'Klavdiya, Kirill, I'm quite impossibly mortified,' Chestnut-Mane began dramatically. 'Sasha wanted so desperately to come, poor man, but they've called him in advance of the reception to confer, and so here I am alone, and I can't stay to dinner and really must dash.'

'No matter, Galina, you are welcome for as long as you can stay.'

Galina helped herself liberally to *zakuski* and drained a tall glass of *Mukuzani*. Then she turned to Ashweald.

'Now, Nikolay Karlovich, tell me about yourself.'

'Ah, Galina Mikhaylovna, what shall I say? That I am in the Soviet Union for the first time in my life, and am greatly impressed.'

'Did I hear Klavdiya say you were English?' The question came through a mouthful of pistachio nuts. 'One would not think it.'

A German, a Frenchman, an American might have puffed out his chest, pocketed the compliment as no more than his due and proceeded to assert his incomparable mastery of the language to the point of some catastrophic howler. Ashweald could find nothing to say.

'You are doubtless Russian by ancestry.'

'I'm afraid not. I owe everything to a student enthusiasm

for phonetics.'

'Your *first* visit, you say? How is that?'

'Lack of opportunity.'

'How good that you have overcome that obstacle. You must come to us and meet my husband.'

'Who is our Ambassador in Dublin,' Klavdiya threw in.

'How do you like Dublin, Galina Mikhaylovna?'

'As a Leningrader I feel entirely at home there. It has some small similarities with this city. Also it is an excellent centre of culture – drama especially – and for shopping.'

The two-piece, the polka-dot silk blouse, the stockings, the stiletto-heeled shoes, Ashweald thought, perhaps also the gold pendant earrings. 'Do you go often to the Abbey Theatre?'

'As often as I can. I admire the Irish dramatists.'

'In spite of the Irish idiom?'

'*Because of it.* I am a student of English. Phonetics is an enthusiasm of mine also. I find no difficulty with variants of Southern Irish, but I can't yet detect the Ulster accent as unerringly as I would like. But tell me,' she continued in an undertone, 'that lady, is she also English?'

Eleanor had just uttered an *O, da*, exactly in the manner of *Oh, yes*, but affectedly and drawn out beyond all rhyme or reason.

'So there we have it,' Galina continued, 'the power of phonetics. Either we bow to it, and all is well. Or we neglect it, and all is not . . . Do you know, Nikolay Karlovich, earlier this week, I met a returned émigré, someone who left England where he had been brought up by Russian parents, oh, ten or fifteen years ago. He's been back here all that time, and yet his Russian is still as English as yours is not . . . '

The small talk continued for a good hour and a good many glasses of *Mukuzani* before Galina remembered her reception. Kirill asked if he should ring for a taxi.

'Thank you, but I have a chauffeur waiting.' She extended a hand to Ashweald which he was tempted to kiss but

35

contented himself with shaking. 'Dear Nikolay Karlovich, you must come to us without fail. Thursday is our day. Three-thirty to eight. Accept my card. But this coming week we shall be in the Crimea.'

'This reception,' Kirill's voice could be heard in the corridor, 'in whose honour is it?'

'I shall remember when I get there – *Hoo Flung Dung, U Bum* – creatures of that sort.' The contempt in her voice was unmistakable.

Kirill returned with a bounce in his step and a broad grin on his broad face. 'Now we can be ourselves. Come through to the dining-room and eat . . . But first I must . . . '

From the carrier bag which Eleanor had presented with the flowers he drew a number of paperbacks, histories of the Soviet Union published in the last few years and works on economics. As he read each title he kissed the cover reverently, before slipping the book behind those already on the shelf.

'Our real library is not for show.' He motioned Ashweald to precede him through the door. 'For show, we display the meretricious, purchased by the metre.'

'You don't mean these?' Ashweald pointed to a great array of mathematical titles in several languages.

'No. They're our bread and butter. My wife and I are scientists, marine architects . . . What I mean are the products of socialist realism . . . But let me introduce you to my mother . . . '

The old lady took his hand in a firm grip and gave a smile of genuine pleasure. She made conventional remarks in a strong clear voice, then concentrated on the task of making a good meal. The linen, the silver, the cut-glass, the fine dinner service which she appeared to take for granted as an everyday phenomenon, were very likely hers, reminders, like the magnificent table and chairs, of a former home, a former order. When she lifted her eyes from her plate, it was to gaze out to where the orange streaks of departing day were dissolving in a deepening blue. For a moment she would sit absorbed in the spectacle, then, roused by the talk at table, continue eating, her face wearing the contentedly indulgent expression of mothers at children's parties.

Ashweald and Eleanor performed the difficult feat of doing justice to the spread while attempting to answer a never-ending stream of questions. *Eleanora Robertovna, Nikolay Karlovich, what do you British think lay behind Stalin's non-aggression pact with Hitler? Tell us, what sort of man you think the American President really is. What is the attitude of ordinary people in England towards nuclear weapons?* And between eating and drinking, Ashweald made a mental note to ask Eleanor on the way home whether Klavdiya and Kirill always dined so well, being privileged to buy from special shops, or whether they had lavished a great deal of time and energy on queueing in their visitors' honour.

When they could eat no more they were served with tea. Not knowing what to do with the bowl of cherry jam he was handed, Ashweald passed it to the grandmother, who scooped a large dollop onto her plate, from which she took spoonfuls between draughts of tea. And now, sitting back and taking a general interest in the scene at the table, the old lady suddenly spoke.

'It is good,' she said slowly and distinctly, 'to hear Russian spoken as once it was, simply and without words that do not signify. With us not much has changed in the real sense, but the language has. What is heard on the wireless and the television receivers seldom pleases.'

The grandmother's Russian was the most beautiful Ashweald had ever heard, and he wished she would go on speaking all night, but Kirill proposed that the men should withdraw for cognac, leaving the ladies to their talk. Klavdiya welcomed this suggestion with an enthusiasm savouring of premeditation. Kirill, to Klavdiya's evident displeasure, begged a handful of cigarettes from Eleanor and conducted Ashweald to the study. Here he poured generous measures of cognac, then lit a cigarette fussily and clumsily, like a man unused to smoking.

'Nikolay Karlovich,' he waved the smoke away from his eyes, 'we have subjected *you* to cross-questioning. Now it must be your turn. Ask away. Be as frank, as critical as you wish.'

Ashweald declined the gambit. He had, he said, been only a short time in the Soviet Union, and so Kirill must not take it amiss if he asked about only a little. No doubt he would have more to ask about later. So he asked about the grandmothers, the *babushki*, who sweep Nevsky Prospekt using besoms of two or three worn twigs; about the unspeakable state of public lavatories; about the shortage of books and the shortage of food. Yes, there *were* such things, Kirill said, but there were also difficulties. Why not overcome the difficulties, Ashweald insisted gently. It could not have been exactly easy to build a metro system in sandy soil, or restore the magnificence of buildings, palaces and gardens, laid waste by the Germans. Kirill lit a second cigarette more inexpertly than the first and again waved away the smoke.

'Nikolay Karlovich, you put it in a nutshell. To do *new* things – build a metro, send men into the cosmos – that is within our powers. To recreate the destroyed – that is also within our powers, supremely so. What is *not* within our powers is to do anything about anything long-established – the depressed condition of the masses, the fact that women have always swept Nevsky Prospekt and suffered doing it, our stagnant economy, the state of lavatories . . .

'I will tell you something . . .' He crouched forward, more like a player about to receive a serve than deliver one. 'Klavdiya and I spend holidays travelling Russia. We take river steamers especially. We travel comfortably and expensively, but this we can do because we are well paid. On these trips we meet other people who are well paid and better paid than we – government functionaries in prominent positions, well-known people. On board we are thrown together, we muck in together, we talk . . . '

He took a long draw at his cigarette, holding it near the unlit end between forefinger and thumb. 'We see much. We hear much. And not all of it comes from the same side of the fence. Not all of it is a re-hash of what *Pravda* says on the subject, or of what Comrade Minister wrote in his annual report. I say this to indicate that Klavdiya and I know not only our own speciality, but also the country, the ruling classes and their attitudes.' Another long draw and much waving away of smoke.

'Over the last ten or twelve years I have kept detailed travel notes. I am now beginning to shape them. They add up to something of interest. But they are too frank ever to find publication here. What I want to ask is whether such notes might find acceptance for publication in the West.' He waited in silence, his cigarette forgotten.

'I think it possible. Only what publishers like is a marketing angle – scandal, persecution of the writer – failing which, information concerning the writer which is bound, when it filters back, to lead to trouble.'

Kirill stubbed out the half-smoked cigarette untidily and lit another. 'I have thought of all that.'

Why do you ask me about this? was the question that suggested itself, but Ashweald thought it prudent to conceal his mistrust. 'You must, I'm sure, have met foreigners better able to advise you than I.'

'In fact, I have not. Or if I have, I have not known whether to trust them.'

'Why should you trust me?'

'Because we know and trust dear Eleanora Robertovna. OK, she has, between you and me, annoying qualities. She is inclined to blurt out, when to keep silent would be better. But she is a person of quality, of judgement. She tells me you have published excellent translations from Russian. I shall need a translator. She says that you are not a British communist or a socialist. That reassures me.'

'Does *she* know about your travel notes?'

He shook his head. 'There is much that we do not tell Eleanora Robertovna. That is part of it.'

'How would you get your manuscript to England?'

'I believe it could be done.'

'And without risk of detection?'

'One would take certain measures.'

'Do you ever think of emigrating?'

'Of defecting, do you mean?' He laid his cigarette on the ashtray and leant forward, hands on knees. 'Nikolay Karlovich, I am, in the final analysis, a patriot.'

'Yet you consider smuggling out criticism of your country to be published and exploited abroad.'

'Paradoxically, yes. All right, I travel the country, as I've told you. Why? Not because I'm curious. Not because I want to amass damaging facts for capitalists to grow fat on. I travel because I must. I love what I see. And because I love it, I can never see enough. The old street sweepers – they deserve compassion, yes, but they are part of what I love and could never leave. They remind me that in Dostoyevsky's time sweeping the Nevsky was a punishment for prostitutes. Now it is still an economic necessity, but the women are no longer prostitutes.'

'Is that of any comfort to the old women?'

'No. No more than Dostoyevsky's compassion for the horse beaten to death was of comfort to the horse. I am not Dostoyevsky. I do not even say with Uncle Vanya that I *might* have been. But I do have a sense of mission. I want to create awareness. In the West. For, one day, when my generation comes into power, it will be important for us to be properly understood, not seen as a worse threat than at present.'

'Do you, like Dostoyevsky, have a faith?'

'Not in God, but in man and man's intelligence. I believe, in the teeth of all the evidence to the contrary, that it is *not* beyond man's power to correct the many imbalances, to lighten the burden of abominable suffering – not eliminate it altogether, for to hope to do that would be naive – but reduce it significantly.'

'And you believe you know how?'

'I *know* I know,' Kirill said with finality, and retrieving his cigarette from the ashtray, puffed without enjoyment.

Ashweald thought of Eleanor's conspirators, Zhelyabov, Perovskaya and the others. They too had *known* . . . 'May I ask what, as a marine architect, you design?' he asked, to change the subject.

'For your ears, which is to say not for Eleanora Robertovna's, Klavdiya and I work in a team concerned with modern submarines.'

'Which must be another reason why you do not consider emigrating.'

'I suppose so. Although it is not the main one. I must say, if I had the choice I would rather design racing yachts. Then it would be easier for me to travel abroad.'

'You never feel tempted in the manner of the MIG-pilots?'

'The MIG-pilots?'

'In the Korean War, the Americans offered a million dollars to the pilot who would desert to them, bringing the latest mark of MIG aircraft. Several did.'

'I call that a form of prostitution. It brings immediate profit, but cannot lead to long-term good. Some disease of the mind, some equivalent of the venereal variety, will intervene to curtail enjoyment and cause regrets.'

'Yes, that is true,' Ashweald said, secretly wondering whether Sue would, in fact, have welcomed Kirill as an ally.

'Nikolay Karlovich, what I propose is this: you take a chapter of my *Travel Notes* with you this evening and study them, when you have time, from a strictly western point of view. Are they of general value, general interest, or are they not? If you think they are, then we can discuss it further.'

So there they were: *White* Martov USSR, *Black* Ashweald GB. Opening: *Tentative Gambit declined*. Black's need, at this

41

advanced stage of play, was to find a reply to achieve equality in the endgame.

'I wish I could – I should very much like to – but they wouldn't be safe, your notes, at the hostel.'

'Ah, you may be right . . . In that case, you will have to come here, or to our *dacha* . . . Supposing you give us a ring. I'll write down our number, and the date we shall return from consultation in Moscow . . . '

'What does Kirill do?' Ashweald asked Eleanor as they walked beside the Griboyedov Canal.

'He's a mathematician. So's Klavdiya. I think they work in some government department.'

'I enjoyed meeting them. Do they always eat as well as that?'

'I imagine so. They seem at a pretty high level of privilege.'

'How did you get those books past the customs?'

'Usual way, Nicholas dear. Scattered among my things. Actually, they're rather lenient with groups like ours, unless they've reason to be suspicious . . . Klavdiya, by the way, was much intrigued to know where you learnt so much Russian. I told her Cambridge and agreed they were good at language teaching – though you know and I know they're the bloody reverse . . . What *did* you do after Cambridge, as a matter of interest?' She had put away an incredible amount of alcohol in the course of the evening, yet her head seemed clearer and her mind sharper than usual.

'I had a spell at the Vienna Embassy as interpreter–translator. I got practice dealing with the Russians there during National Service. Then I had four years in Germany. Same sort of work.'

'Foreign Office?'

'Yes.'

'Not TOF?'

'TOF?'

'Abbreviation.'

'Not one I know.'

'Oh look – the beauty of the reflections! Something I've never done all the times I've been here is to look down on a canal from high up – from a window like that one which keeps shattering into slivers of light on the water . . . ' She took his arm as they walked slowly on. 'What years', she asked apropos of nothing, 'were you in Austria?'

'I'm getting weak on dates. Early fifties, I suppose.'

'So you coincided with Peter.'

'Peter?'

'Peter Lomax Gray, dear. Him as got fifty-six years for spying, only to vanish like a puff of smoke from that Isle of Wight place I never remember the name of.'

'I must have read about it.'

'Never came across him?'

'No,' Ashweald lied.

'Some say he was helped to escape and that he's now *somewhere in Russia*, as the phrase is.'

'Really?'

'But in that case you'd expect him to have been spotted by now or wheeled out on show.'

'I suppose so.' Pause. 'Did *you* know him?'

'I knew someone who knew him,' Eleanor said with only a trace of hesitation before coughing violently. 'Still, if he is here I can't say I envy him . . . '

'Why not?'

'Would you, after spying for the buggers in an ecstasy of idealism, want to spend the rest of your life savouring the drab reality of an unworkable system?'

'I suppose, as an idealist, I'd retain a certain optimism and make the best of a bad job.'

'You mean you'd be happy to spend the rest of your life here?'

'If by here you mean Leningrad,' he said lightly, 'I think I might.'

Eleanor looked Ashweald fully in the face, and in the

43

neutral, jollying tone of a girls' housemistress, exclaimed 'Good for you.'

Carvel was entertaining Helen Blore, whose Russian boy-friend had gone to his sick father in Vilnius, spoiling the dirty weekend they had planned. From the tenor of Carvel's remarks, Ashweald judged that it might well be in Carvel's mind to make up to Helen for what she was missing. He switched to Eleanor's radio microphone.

'Nice evening?' The voice was Tatiana's.

'Absolutely marvellous. Now what would you like? There's vodka, whisky or cognac.'

'I think, at this hour, a small cognac.'

'Wonder if Irina would like a night-cap?'

'She's not in.'

'Not in?'

'Gone to Repino to see a girl she studied with in Moscow. If she misses the last train she'll have to spend the night.'

''Gainst rules . . .'

'But rules are made . . .'

He switched off, took his stick and let himself out.

'*A vy kuda, molodoy chelovek* – And where are you off to, young man?' A *dezhurnaya* he had not seen before, materialized out of the shadowed reception area he had thought empty.

'I feel like a walk before turning in.'

'It is very late for a walk.'

'But a good time to admire your city by moonlight.'

She gave a smile that confirmed the irony intended by her *young man*. 'Hope you enjoy our city by moonlight.'

For a good half hour he stood at the head of the escalator in the Nevsky Prospekt metro station, hoping to see Irina amongst those rising into view. The waits between groups of arrivals grew longer, the groups themselves grew smaller, and wherever he positioned himself, an old lady came sweeping with a three-twig besom. Time, he decided, to stop making a fool of himself and go.

Outside, under the station portico, a group of young people were lying or lolling, listening with rapt attention to one of their number who was coaxing from a guitar what sounded like intricate variations on Shostakovich's musical signature.

Never had he seen the Nevsky so empty. At the far end, pending the return of the sun, floodlights were directed on the golden Admiralty Spire. The ankle felt easier. He would walk to People's Bridge, *Narodny most*, cross over and go home to bed. The implacable heat of the day was now balmy warmth. The moon was full.

What an evening it had been. Eleanor was pulling ahead of Carvel in the suspects' stakes. Only employees of the Old Firm ever referred to it as TOF, and then strictly amongst their own kind. To employ it as something between an identification signal and a Freemason's handshake was, in the jargon, a gross breach of security. And the lead about Peter . . . Something else that evening had put him in mind of Peter. *Our tricky friend* – no, that had been Archie . . . Whatever it was, now refused to come to mind. Thoughts that did that were like cats, best left to return in their own good time.

Nevsky Prospekt! How often he had read of others walking it, or corrected translations of Gogol's effusion! Now *he* was walking where Gogol and Dostoyevsky walked, and the sheer wonder of it was something that would never diminish. We Russians do not *need* to drink, he remembered a friend saying, for to be a Russian is to be in a state of permanent intoxication with life and its beauty! He felt he understood even better now.

And just when the beauty of the moonlit Nevsky was at its most intoxicating, a figure emerged from an archway on the other side of the avenue, a figure whose walk was familiar. He

45

made as if to cross, was on the point of calling her name, then noticed she was not alone. A man was at her side. He was talking, she was listening, head lowered as she walked. Ashweald marked the archway: last building before Moyka Embankment and People's Bridge, under which he and Irina had watched the motor-boat disappear.

He turned about and kept pace with them, eight traffic lanes and two generous pavement-widths distant. The man striding evenly beside Irina, absorbed in what he had to say, seemed a mocking counterpart of Ashweald himself. His manner of shaking hands, a ritual he performed stiffly and formally at the turning where only a short walk separated Irina from the hostel, accentuated the parody. The man went back the way he had come. Ashweald kept Irina in sight, but did not attempt to catch up with her.

# 4.

Ashweald woke with a start. The squeaky flight of a mosquito was what woke him, and there was nothing for it but to get up and direct a burst of insect repellant at the net curtains. He regretted, not for the first time, his failure to connect *Neva* with the implications of its origin in the Finnish for *marsh*. Had he done so, he would have included with the month's supply of toilet paper, soap, washing powder, etc., a reliable defence against mosquitoes. The next best thing, purchased of the chemist's by Stone Bridge, belched forth a treacly cloud redolent of creosote and low-grade petrol, which ran a good second to atomic fall-out in the time it took to dissipate. While waiting, he dabbed his freshly-bitten wrists and knuckles with disinfectant and checked his radio microphones. Eleanor was snoring. Carvel, well, Carvel was speaking sleepily and apparently into his pillow, and what he said refused to arrange itself in the mind as sense until the girlish giggle that followed. *The wages of sex, my dear, is a need to wee . . .*

'What if I meet Nick Ashweald on the way?' That was Helen Blore. He switched off, hoping that when the time came, the English of the monitor of the Russian bug, if any, would prove equal to the task of transcription.

He gave Irina till eight before setting off to the *Visla*, feeling, he knew unreasonably, irritated and let down, a mood intensified at the *Visla* by having to queue and watch the items he hoped to breakfast off, dwindling behind their glass. And the

47

less she had to sell, the more attentive and ruthlessly efficient the buxom blonde became.

'*Bud'te zdorovy* . . . '

'*Blagodaryu vas* . . . '

He carried his coffee and single slice of black bread to where Carvel sat. Carvel, rosy and rested, greeted him with a smile.

'Care to miss Chichibayev this morning? Ted and Terry's suitcases got delivered to Vienna instead of Moscow. They ought by now to be with Austrian Air in Moscow. The lads have done their best to organize the next move, using English and Russian, and so have I, but still no cases. What's needed is for someone to ring and say *what the hell* in German. You, Nick, are our only German speaker . . . I'll square things and give you a shout about nine. There's a post office in Plekhanov Street where we can book a call.'

'I could phone home at the same time.'

'Not from there. *The* place is at the Admiralty end of the Nevsky, almost opposite the *Beryozka*. It's specially for foreign tourists, and the service is quick.'

Ashweald ate his slice of dry bread and Carvel stared out at the brightly sunlit façades on the other side of the Moyka.

'I think I'll tell Chichibayev we may have to go out to Pulkovo and miss the whole morning.'

'Good idea.'

'Mustn't miss the visit to the Piskaryov Memorial Cemetery after lunch, though.'

The problem of the cases was quickly solved, and they went their separate ways: Carvel in a taxi, with a regal flourish; Ashweald on foot and with difficulty through the crowd.

The building from which he had seen Irina come was finely proportioned and discreetly ornamented. The archway was unguarded, and once through, he had the impression of slipping, as if by magic, out of a swirling, clamorous torrent into a placid backwater. The abruptness of the calm had a shock effect. It was like plunging into an icy pool. What composed the calm and radiated it generally was the little garden of grass, shrubs and trees, contained and overlooked by the four green-washed baroque façades. The shapely wrought-iron railings enclosing the garden were as perfectly appropriate as those of the city's embankments and bridges. Of the trees, one particular birch, its delicate leaves shining all shades of green in the slanting sun, veiling and mottling a classical statue, made him catch his breath in astonishment. Nature and art in perfect harmony. Perhaps it was the key to the charm of Leningrad that nature and art *did* harmonize more often and more significantly than in any other city of Europe. Keeping to the pavement, he made a slow round of the square, reminded of Austrian *Hofs*, Cambridge courts and the cathedral closes where clerics and solicitors nest.

To the right of the archway, where he had not seen him on entering, a painter sat before an easel, intent, it might be supposed, on immortalizing the symmetry of façade, railings and statue amidst the chaotic light-dark patterns created by sun-shafted foliage. He made another round of the square, this time taking a line that would enable him to look over the painter's shoulder.

The birch – *his* birch – was central to the conception, as receiver and transmitter of light, as obscurer and illuminator, as filter . . . The rest was already indicated, and at the base of the tree, even in some detail. But the birch, its leaves, its tiny brittle branchlets – they were what had to be managed to perfection if they were to animate the canvas as they did the actual scene. And this was what was happening, and with a zest of conscious and confident achievement that was apparent in the very manner of patting on the golden green flecks with the knife . . .

He would have liked to make a third circuit, would have liked to talk to the artist, but fearful of interrupting, he went on his way.

To the Piskaryov Cemetery they travelled in an Intourist coach with an Intourist guide who, as they swung this way and that through the traffic, commented on points of interest along the route. These were many, and in the glare and heat of the afternoon the background mutter of British voices soon gave way to sleepy silence. Ashweald approved of the guide, who was a student on vacation. She did her job well, evidently trying not to weary or bore. From time to time, Ted and Terry, now resplendent in navy-blue blazers with college crests, would consult her, leaning, rigidly attentive, over the back of her seat, while she, a veritable Pythia, gave answer, smiling engagingly, microphone held as if for an interview, but switched off.

Irina was sitting some distance away at the back of the bus. He had been hoping they would sit together, but she had boarded before him and got well and truly squashed in by the bulk of Ernie Oldroyd. Prior to the onset of sleepy silence, he had heard Ernie complaining he did not understand one word of what yon guide was yammering about and demanding that Irina translate.

At the cemetery Ashweald broke away from the rest of the party and walked alone between the expanses of grass which now mark the mass graves. He felt a need to form thoughts. But what could be thought, what could be said, even in one's own mind, in the presence of the remains of four hundred and seventy thousand fellow beings, knowing them to be only *some* of those killed by German action or starvation or disease or the cold during the siege of Leningrad . . . Tears formed, but not thoughts . . . And with the tears came a remembered fact. To this place it was that Olga Bergholz had dragged her husband's body on a child's toboggan through the snow. In January 1942. Earlier that month she had written those lines about the Red Army man so stirred to pity by a mother and her children that he gives the children his last crust. Their mother – like another woman, in the Gospel – touches the sleeve of his greatcoat. Her hand is smoke grey. Ablaze with shame – the shame of father, man and soldier – the Red Army man walks on. Behind him, in the grey rays of the January sunset, the great city lies dying . . .

Ashweald's own son had written of a visit here, and in a style quite unlike his usual matter-of-factness. *We were at the Cemetery*, his postcard ran, *where many of the million and a half of those who died or were killed in the Siege are buried. The huge area of grass is like scar tissue – living, tidy, but appalling evidence still of a colossal, near-mortal wound. That wound you glimpse as it must have been . . . And standing there, you dimly understand . . .*

*HERE LIE LENINGRADERS.*
*HERE ARE PEOPLE OF THE CITY –*
*MEN, WOMEN, CHILDREN.*
*AT THEIR SIDE, SOLDIERS OF THE RED ARMY.*
*THEY WITH THEIR ALL*
*DEFENDED YOU, LENINGRAD,*
*CRADLE OF THE REVOLUTION.*
*THEIR ILLUSTRIOUS NAMES WE CANNOT HERE NUMBER,*
*SO MANY ARE THEY IN THE KEEPING OF ETERNAL GRANITE.*
*BUT KNOW, YOU WHO HEED THESE STONES,*
*NO ONE, AND NOTHING, IS FORGOTTEN.*

Those words of Olga Bergholz, like her poem, told the simple truth. And having read and re-read them as best he could through blurring tears, he turned away from the memorial, and followed the least peopled of the parallel paths.

'Ah, young man . . . ' The voice penetrated to him from afar, an old, old voice, the classic Russian old woman's voice of radio, film and reality. 'Ah, young man, we have seen sorrow in our day . . . '

She was sitting alone on one of the severely simple benches, a Russian old lady in black – small, indestructible, face sere, tearless and vital, counterpart of Kirill's mother, of so many Russian mothers.

'True, mother,' he answered, his voice not his own. 'True, mother, true . . . '

That was what he said, and there was a kind of appropriateness about it. But nothing that he personally had endured could, he knew, amount to more than the merest fraction of what she suffered here daily, some forty years ago, as a young woman, for so many of the nine hundred days of the Siege.

He wiped his eyes with a handkerchief grimy from imperfect washing and days of brow-mopping. Compassion had to be controlled, channelled, assuaged – by good works, by monetary contribution . . . To let it thrive uncontrolled and unchannelled was beyond human endurance. Time to play the man, rejoin the others. No. He would tell Carvel he'd rather walk. The coach, the need to talk as if inwardly intact, inwardly unshattered – that was more than he could face.

Someone was coming. The old woman, he thought, the steps were so hesitant, so craintive. It was Irina. He did his best to smile. She put a hand to his elbow, as if to set him on course. Together they walked in silence towards the gates.

'I was going to tell Carvel I would rather walk,' he said.

'Let me walk with you. I won't talk.'

Her face wore a look he had not seen before – hard, set and intense, the very opposite of his own shapeless, incoherent emotion.

The most direct way back to their side of the river was by Liteyny Bridge, but they went adrift, or rather Ashweald did and Irina with him, passing near the Cruiser *Aurora* without even noticing it. So it was that they crossed the Neva by Kirov Bridge and were exposed to a vast and magnificent panoramic sweep of river, from the Peter and Paul Fortress on their right, via St Isaac's golden dome, to the Winter Palace on their left. It burst on them simultaneously,

52

bringing them to a halt, and they stood and stared in incredulous admiration.

> *'I stood in Venice, on the Bridge of Sighs:*
> *A Palace and a prison on each hand.'*

She spoke the words in an undertone, almost apologetically, as if reluctant to break her promise.

'Byron?'

'Byron.'

'Who we don't read, and clearly should . . . '

'It's not really so apt. In Venice it's all pinched together, the exact reverse of this. The prison's only a few steps from the palace – you can hear and see the one from the other very clearly . . . But I expect you know.'

'I've never been to Venice.'

'My goodness!' She looked suddenly alarmed as the bridge vibrated beneath a cluster of buses. 'Do you think it's safe?'

'Let's move on, in case it isn't.'

As they walked upstream with the breeze at their backs it seemed suddenly hotter. The air was full of shrieking, circling, side-slipping gulls. A little boy was standing on the parapet throwing pellets of bread to be caught in mid-air. Mother and father each had hold of a foot and seemed to be pressing it to the granite.

'That's something you could see by the Thames or any river you can think of,' he said.

'I can remember being held just like that.'

'Feeding the gulls, I meant. I've never seen a child held like that before – isn't it peculiarly Russian?'

'I wouldn't have thought so.'

Across the road the railings of The Summer Garden were beginning, *the best in the world*, Akhmatova calls them in her poem, and so they are – delicate, almost ethereal, between their lofty, urn-surmounted pillars, whether you look out through them at the river and sky, or in at the trees and statues.

As they waited to cross Irina said, 'I'm sorry I overslept this morning.'

'I missed you at breakfast.'

'I missed you at lessons. I couldn't think what had happened to you.'

'I had to telephone in German.'

'And are poor Ted and Terry to get their change of linen?'

'They've got it already.'

'And that took you all the morning?'

'We played truant. I looked at bookshops. Bought beer at a *Beryozka*, cheese at a *gastronom*, bread from Herzen Street, oh, and a new tall jar of pickled gherkins, also from Herzen Street. And I phoned home.'

'Your wife must have been glad to hear from you.'

'My wife is dead. It was my daughter I rang. She's looking after the dog and the cat and the tortoises – our prehistoric sheep. My son's abroad.'

'You see, I *should* have kept quiet . . . '

'I'm glad you didn't . . . '

It was the simple truth. His greatest need was for a woman's company, a woman's voice. Not the company and the voice of any woman, but of a woman in a hundred thousand, such as Sue had been, such as Irina would be for the man she married . . .

'Come on, now's our chance.'

On the other side, they stood and looked at the railings close to.

'Nicholas . . . '

From the seriousness of her voice and her hesitation he half expected a confidence to follow, or a confession.

' . . . When Akhmatova says in that poem she's going to look at the roses, then admires the railings, then jumps from one thing to another, forgetting the roses – do you think she knows what she's doing?'

He laughed. 'Maybe she remembers that once you could walk here only at the Tsar's invitation . . . The flitting may just be breathless delight at actually going where she has no right to expect to be.'

'Like us.'

'Like us.'

They walked from statue to statue along the main avenue beneath the sun-dappled shade of the limes. They turned aside to look at Krylov's, ornamented with the creatures of his fables. The garden was full of parents walking children or pushing them in chairs or sitting with them, apparently in serious conversation. It was a place where the ordinary and everyday was transformed to a point just short of seeming ordinary and everyday – as if the focusing knob of the camera refused to sharpen up reality and left it agreeably fuzzy. Loth to leave, they sat on a bench not far from the Carp Pond. It was pleasant to sit, after walking so far in the heat, but it was hard not to doze.

'I spy,' he said, recoiling from the very brink of sleep, 'I spy an Englishman and his lady . . .'

She followed his gaze. 'How can you be so sure – at this distance?'

'I *am* sure. English as you or I. And what he's probably saying in that avuncular fashion is what wouldn't he give for a cup of well-mashed tea and a slice of toast and dripping – beef dripping, with a nice pinch of salt.'

'Rubbish. I'm going to call your bluff.'

'Bet you the price of tomorrow's breakfast I'm right.'

'Bet you the price of a *week* of breakfasts you're wrong.'

'Taken.'

He watched her go, and if, in those few moments, Mephistopheles had flopped down beside him, he would have struck any bargain to shed twenty years – to be thirty again . . . To brush a cheek against that hair . . . Through half-closed eyes he watched her pass slowly behind the bench in question, pause to look at a statue. Then she came back. Even crestfallen, she walked with poise.

'You cheated. You know them by sight.'

'I don't.'

'Then tell me how you knew.'

'By the pipe. English is the only language you can speak with a pipe in your mouth. I know. I used to smoke one.'

She laughed, a merry, incredulous laugh. He averted his eyes from the blue-flecked grey of hers. 'And was the talk of tea?'

'It was, damn you.'

'Come and have some with me at the *Astoriya*.'

'Sure you want me to?'

'Quite sure.'


'Care to join me in a Lager or two?' Carvel called as Ashweald passed his open door. 'Bring your tooth glass.'

He had felt less warmly towards Carvel since the evidence that his honesty and sincerity might simply be tools – a means to an end – but he determined not to show it. In his Old-Firm days he would have accepted instantly and without question that any detail gleaned from playing voyeur, must, by its very nature, be more reliable than anything observed from day-to-day contact with people busily acting a part. Now he could no longer be sure. Carvel might be less black than he seemed, or blacker.

Carvel filled Ashweald's tooth glass and pushed several unopened cans along the dressing table in his direction, rather in the manner of a croupier dispensing chips. 'Quite a march from the cemetery in this heat . . . Cheers . . . '

'Cheers.'

'You seem to get on well with Irina.'

'She's very good company.'

'Speaks good Russian.'

'Amazingly good.'

'What plans for this evening?'

'River trip, probably.'

'Becoming a habit. Oh, by the by, Ted and Terry looked in to express their gratitude. I undertook to convey it.'

'Nice of them.'

'Proper toffs now they've got their kit.'

'So I saw.'

Carvel drained his glass and pulled the hand-grenade ring of another can. '*You* weren't one, were you?'

'Homosexual?'

'No, of course not.' He gestured violently at the ceiling, cupped a hand to an ear and whispered, 'Tell you when we're clear of the Big Brother atmosphere.'

Ashweald nodded vaguely.

'Know, don't you, old boy, *why* they call us TOF?' had been a favourite question of Warburton's. 'Initial letters?' the victim would hazard. 'No, no, no. FO – Foreign Office – reversed. *They* weave away like Penelope at father-in-law's robe. *We* unpick the bloody thing when they've gone to bed . . .'

So Carvel was aware of the bugging danger. Why then did he encourage some visitors to talk as if that danger did not exist?

# 5.

In the Director's sanctum, contrasting oddly with the sporting prints on the wall behind the Director's head, had hung a notice in burnt-poker-work of a style more often seen in seaside boarding houses and souvenir shops. On his first day with the Firm, during the Director's tedious speech of welcome, Ashweald had worked at it as one might the lower reaches of an optician's chart, and eventually deciphered:

> *A*
> *secret*
> *shared*
> *is a*
> *hazard*
> *prepared*

'Words we do well to ponder,' the Director said, seeing what he was at. 'They put into a nutshell the First and Basic Law of our line of business. Oh yes. Think of it, er, Ashfield, as a Sword of Damocles suspended over each and every one of us, every minute of every day . . . '

And think of it he did, particularly when he saw people come to grief on hazards of their own preparing. And he noted that the more personal the secret – as against official – the more tempted they were to share it. Which was why he told no one, not even Irina, of the painting he had seen in what he now knew to be the courtyard of the old Stroganov Palace. For if it was for sale, that painting, he was determined to buy it. And if it *was*, and if he *did*, it would still be a long, long haul from the Soviet Union to his study where he wanted it to hang. The artist would want payment in currency other than roubles. That currency would have to be smuggled in on some future visit. The canvas would have to be smuggled out. To risk adding to the already considerable number of hazards would be suicidal.

*Why* he so desperately wanted the painting did not figure so strongly as the bald fact that he *did*. It was love at first sight, an unreasoning desire, an infatuation stimulated by the recognition that already, in its unfinished state, the picture, for him, embodied the essence of Russia – that Russia for which émigrés, refugees, deserters, defectors, expelled dissidents and the rest never ever cease to yearn, because nothing anywhere else in the whole wide world can make up for its loss. That painting *was* Russia, and when his pitifully few weeks of Russia were done, it would have the power instantly to transport him to where he would not again easily find money or opportunity to go.

Meanwhile, the essential next step was to meet up with the painter, but since occasions for slipping away to the Stroganov Palace, alone and at a suitable time of day, were few and far between, and since also the painter seemed to have given up painting there, his growing obsession was becoming suffused with growing anxiety and frustration.

'Nick, dear, you look like a dying duck in a thunder storm. Come and have a nice lot of whisky this very instant.'

'I'd like to, Eleanor, but I'm waiting for Irina.'

'Irina shall have some too.'

'The snag is we're going on the river and want to catch the sun before it goes.'

'Lucky Irina. Wish *I* was going on the Neva.'

'Come this weekend – if you're not going on the Tallinn trip.'

'Oh, but I am. Tallinn's not to be missed. Why aren't you

coming? You'd like Tallinn. Irina is of the party, is she not?'

'I thought I'd stay here and take it easy.'

Eleanor became mock-threatening. 'Naughty man. You're up to something, I know it. I shall voice apprehensions to Irina.'

'Irina knows I behave impeccably. She won't believe you.'

'Oh my, how dull. Never mind. I shall now go and, House Management permitting, have a bath . . . ' At which, the benefit of alcohol plainly upon her, Eleanor proceeded with dignity, making smoke like a dreadnought, her two *Beryozka* carrier bags chinking rhythmically.

Supposing, just *supposing*, Archie had some means of knowing, what would he make of this failure to accompany Carvel and Eleanor to Tallinn? But here was Irina, and where Irina was, neither Archie and his works nor the painting seemed to matter so very greatly.

He travelled on the coach to the station, ostensibly to see the party off, but really to postpone the loneliness of the weekend just a little by keeping company with Irina until the last moment.

It was growing dark as the coach set off. The guide instantly reached for her microphone, and the hearts of all – save possibly Ted, Terry and Ernie – groaned audibly at the prospect of instructive commentary. But after announcing what station they were making for and how long they would take, she put the microphone away, leaving them all to their gloomy silence.

'Sorry you're not coming, Nick,' Irina said, 'it's going to be awfully, awfully dull without you . . . '

'Sorry you're not staying.'

'I dithered . . . But somehow I feel a need to be reminded that a world still exists beyond obsessive, possessive Leningrad . . . '

The quip that came to his lips he left unsaid, so suddenly shrunken, even fearful, did she seem. Her face wore something of the hard, purposefully hard, expression he had seen for an instant at the cemetery. And not for the first time he fell to wondering what it might be, that silent, steely side of her that welcomed no intrusion.

At the Baltic Station there were many similar coaches and a great confusion of comings and goings. Some parties were waiting for luggage to be unloaded from boots, others for it to be loaded; while yet others were simply waiting. Ashweald carried Irina's case until bereft of it by a cheerful porter who swung it up onto the absurdly high pile on his trolley.

'Now just you heed that, young Nick. There's one respect in which the First Socialist State has outstripped us and is on top: porters, my boy, honest-to-God good old-fashioned *porters* . . . Never ever saw one of those in England, eh? Like bananas in the war.'

Ashweald grunted, wishing Ernie would shove off, and was glad when he did. But his gladness dissipated like smoke when he saw Ernie step nimbly as a goat into the same couchette as Irina, Eleanor and Carvel, flourish forth a bottle of claret and a round Dutch cheese from his case, and place them on the little table with Eleanor's litre of Scotch.

'Don't wait for us to pull out,' Irina said, standing with him on the platform.

'Enjoy yourself.'

She squeezed his hand. 'You too.'

At the far end of the platform he gave a last wave of his stick, and assailed by a fresh pang of jealousy, was not sorry to escape into the bright silent warmth of the Leningrad night.

He walked all the way to the hostel and entered it in a cheerless mood which the glinty grittiness of the stairs, the harsh lighting and the icy black-painted iron of the handrail intensified, reminding him of identical stairs in almost identical stairways in barracks, colleges, government offices and the like, of the homesickness and loneliness which once, long, long ago, had gone with them – a reminder as palpable as the whiff of another's cigarette. Up, up, up he climbed, and like forbidding pinnacles on an unfamiliar ridge, loomed Saturday morning, Saturday afternoon, Saturday evening, and beyond, Sunday morning, Sunday afternoon, Sunday evening . . .

The television was dead. Chairs, settees, ashtrays were all empty. The corridor was as deserted as at seven forty-five a.m. when he was wont to sit gazing down it, waiting for Irina. The silence was uncanny. No banging of doors. No hoots of laughter. No music. No singing. No endless flow of broadcast Russian. It was a *Marie Celeste* of a hostel.

He bent to insert his key in the lock, then, alarmed by a slight sound behind him, straightened and swung round. Lady Tatiana carrying an iron and an ironing board was finding difficulty in closing the door of the cleaners' sanctum behind her. He relieved her of both burdens. The ironing board might have been made of teak, the iron itself, of lead.

'Irina does the fetching for me usually . . . I really imagined I was sole survivor . . .'

Her English was thoroughly English, only the timbre of her voice was Russian. She reminded Ashweald of his professor, of all the Anglo-Russian ladies he had ever known, amphibians, at home in two worlds in a way that he could never now be.

Lady Tatiana's room was the exact counterpart of his own and everyone else's, but homelier. An embroidered bedspread, a tablecloth, a samovar, a Persian rug, colourful cushions contributed to the effect and accounted for the weight of her cases. But what, above all, stamped the room with personality were the pencil drawings affixed to most vertical surfaces – portraits of members of the course, scenes of Leningrad, impressions of *objets d'art*. He looked at once for Irina and found her, seated, intensely pensive, back to the wall, on Tatiana's bed beneath the gaze of two Bank Footbridge griffons, the subject of another sketch, faithfully included as in a photograph.

'Yes, there she is . . . Remarkable bone structure – Slav,

pure Slav. Doesn't know her pedigree – or says she doesn't – but I tell you, Nikolay Karlovich, Slav blood runs in Irina Pavlovna's veins . . . But sit yourself down, take under your wing that carafe of vodka . . . No, not for me. For me a little Georgian wine . . . '

The room radiated optimism, security. He had the feeling of coming in from a November evening to a hearth of red-glowing oak and ash, with a dog and a cat stretched out, and muffins keeping hot on a dish . . .

'You don't smoke, Nikolay Karlovich? How I wish dear Eleanor did not. Her company is a delight, but those *yedkiye ispareniya*, or whatever we call them, are not . . . '

'*Acrid emanations?*'

'Exactly. Oh dear. My Russian goes when I am not in Russia, which is most of the time. And when I *am* in Russia, which is not often since it costs so much and I rely on subsidized visits, like the present one, my English goes. It is sad.'

'Don't you find it tedious attending lessons in a language you don't need to learn?'

'No. No more than you, or Irina . . . *Being here* where it is still not easy to get, that is what matters. And our teachers are of the living stream of Russian, which we cannot be . . . '

He smiled. 'You are the voice of reason.'

'You think so? I prefer to make my sermons in the form of drawings, as you see . . . And I would like to add *you* to my collection . . . ' Her gaze was bright and intent and camera-like. 'No need to play the statue. Move, help yourself to vodka as you wish . . . '

The idea of seeing himself as Lady Tatiana saw him seemed agreeable until he fell to examining some of the sketches in front of him more closely.

Her Carvel suggested nothing of Shakespeare. It was as if she had seen beyond the impression with which Ashweald was stuck. Of wisdom, quizzical good humour, self suffi-ciency, he saw no trace. The face was bland, the forehead receding rather than domed, the lips sneeringly, almost cruelly, curled. Or was it a trick of the light? Or to do with a certain couchette swaying rhythmically through the night? Or simply a fact that the character of a face on paper, like the character of a face in the flesh, was a matter of faith?

Eleanor was in her hat with the feather, but looking through half-closed eyes towards the ceiling so that her face was fully revealed. She had a cigarette between her lips, and her eyes might have been following the ascent of the smoke. She had been allowed the wisdom denied to Carvel. It was the face of the thinker, with nothing of drinker . . . A wooden wall-mask, half Einstein, half noble savage . . .

Only Ernie did they seem to see in the same way: chubby, petulant, the eternal bouncing baby. Or was there more of donnish shrewdness than naughty twinkle in the eyes behind their horn-rimmed spectacles?

'Almost finished.'

'Shall I distract you if I talk?'

'Talk away.'

'I was wondering,' he said, as if only idly curious, 'where young Soviet artists market their work . . . '

Why the *young*, he asked himself in the interval of silence that followed his question, for he remembered nothing of the Stroganov Palace artist.

'I suppose through the state . . . But probably privately too. I must confess I've never bought any Soviet art . . . '

'Where would you go if you were thinking of buying?'

'Galleries . . . Exhibitions . . . *Gostiny Dvor*, perhaps . . . I've not looked . . . There must, I'm sure, be official and unofficial open-air exhibitions from time to time . . . I will make some inquiries.'

Next morning he woke at his usual time, and went and filled an empty kilo-sized can with ice-cold water from the red-topped tap in the bathroom. Back in his room, he stood a tiny immersion heater in the can of water and plugged in the lead.

Everyone in the party now had empty cans, having either brought them, complete with contents – peaches, pineapple chunks, grapefruit segments or fruit juices – from England, or run to earth cans of similar size, though with less desirable contents, in the *Beryozki*. Like Colditz, Ernie had once let slip, after stumbling into his own little stock of cans, only to spring instantly to the defence of the system – or lack of it – which reduced foreign visitors to brewing beverages, boiling eggs and heating shaving water in old tins, like so many prisoners of war.

By the time he was dressed the water was boiling. He shaved with care so as not to delay himself dabbing blood. It was seven fifteen when he left the hostel, and less than ten minutes later he entered the courtyard of the Stroganov Palace.

Sunless, it struck cold, and the features he remembered as so especially appealing were now flat and uninteresting. Cars were parked in the square, their windscreens wiperless. The only sound was of a broom sweeping. He made towards the sound. The sweeper was, as he expected, an old woman. He wished her good day but got only a sharp, unfriendly look in return.

'I'm not German,' he said, sensing the reason for her hostility. 'I'm English.'

'English . . . ' The look did not greatly alter. 'One of those we prayed, prayed day and night, would open a Second Front . . . ' She stood, supporting herself on the broom whose handle was as tall as she, stern as a judge and looking, in her headkerchief, not unlike one. 'But you waited, did you not, waited until we had the fascists on the run before landing a tiny army in France. Was it your hope that they would finish us?'

What was he to say? That as a schoolboy, teaching himself her language – often in an air-raid shelter – he had prayed for the Russians to hit back, not seeing how else the Germans could be beaten? That there was as much or as little truth in

65

her view as in his own concerning the Russian delay in liberating Warsaw? That the suffering of her people – like that of the Jews – was an absolute, comparable to nothing, barely comprehensible from the inside, certainly incomprehensible from without?

'No,' he said at last, 'I did not hope that. I have not heard of anyone who did.'

'*We* cannot forget.'

'No, you cannot . . . But may I ask *why* you took me for a German?'

She continued to gaze around her broom at him, but her expression had lost something of its severity. 'By your shoes you are a foreigner. Your bearing is military – Prussian, do you understand? And who but a German would set out to sight-see at such an early hour, or be so thorough as to include this palace in his route?'

And where but in Russia would a woman sweeping pavements talk in this way? But later, remembering how, during the war, American servicemen in Britain made themselves ridiculous by mistaking lords of manors for tramps, he saw the idiocy of judging foreigners by one's own standards, or by any.

'It must attract a great many photographers and artists, this courtyard.'

'Not so many as it deserves. Students come – their professors send them – to draw the lions on the great doors, or the sphinxes there, or the statues . . . '

'I saw an artist here a few days ago, just inside the gateway.'

'With a beard? Timid, like a hare?'

'I can't say. I was interested only in what he was painting.'

'Lomashev, Pyotr Petrovich, often paints here. He is an Honoured Artist of the Soviet Union. You will see his work in *Gostiny Dvor*.'

The leap of encouragement he felt at having a name to juggle with became a plunge of despair at the thought that if he were well known he might be painting to special commission. His work might easily not be for sale.

'Can you tell me where in *Gostiny Dvor* his work is?'

'Walking from here, it is almost the last window in the arcade before you come to Sadovaya Street.'

The Lomashev reproductions displayed in *Gostiny Dvor* were chocolate-box stuff in frames of assorted sizes: the Pushkin Monument against summer green, autumn gold and winter white; the Bronze Horseman against a nasty coppery orange sunset or dawn; avenues reminiscent of Versailles and Schönbrunn, with and without fallen leaves; ornate fountains, mournful seascapes . . . The sort of thing he associated with glossies like *Ogonyok* and *Sovyetsky Soyuz*. The painter of those could hardly be the painter of the Stroganov courtyard.

And so it was that when, later that morning, he returned to the courtyard at roughly the same time as on his very first visit and saw, with surprise and excitement, a man at an easel in the same position as before, his one thought was to check whether the painting really was as good as he had thought it. If not, the whole thing could be forgotten. He'd be rid of a nagging obsession, free of an aberration brought about by the magic of the city . . . Either way, his quest was nearly done. The rest of the day he could sunbathe on the Gulf of Finland, as the buxom blonde had recommended at breakfast. Such were his thoughts as he walked around the square, intending to approach as before and take a look over the artist's shoulder . . .

He seemed to hear a voice, a voice saying *Bloody Ashweald!* over and over, but his only reaction – an almost subconscious one at that – was mild surprise at an obvious error . . . *Archie*, it should have been, *Bloody Archie* . . .

The palette knife was held curiously, more like a dagger than a tool, but Ashweald merely registered the fact, not connecting it with himself, and kept walking. There it was, his golden fleece – the obverse of it. A few steps more and he would know if the gold were genuine. Then, suddenly, his way was barred. The immediate shock of finding his way barred was no worse than that of treading on a stair not there, but the next instant, to his horror, a madman dashed at him. Ashweald swung sideways, grabbed the arm terminating in the knife-clenching fist and pulled, at the same time extending a foot. It was a response practised in the army but never put to practical use. The result was immediate and alarming: his assailant fell hard and lay where he fell. *Then, when he's down* . . . the robot voice of the unarmed combat instructor squeaked again in Ashweald's head, detailing *how to hurt the enemy good and proper* . . . But this was not war. The man was not an enemy. The man was winded and in pain. Ashweald helped him to his feet, supported him to the camp stool before the easel. He had never knocked anyone down with his car, but at that moment he had some idea of what it must be like, walking back to face the mess.

'I'm sorry,' he said lamely, 'I really thought you were going to knife me . . . '

The man gulped painfully for air, and after a while said, equally lamely, 'Yes . . . I think I was . . . '

Ashweald retrieved the palette knife from the gutter. He laid it on a ledge of the easel. The picture had advanced little, but he saw that he had been right in his judgement of it.

'Why – *why* – have – you – come? Why?'

The words were an intrusion, the dispelling of a dream world whose warming, illuminating, benevolent sun was compounded of beauty, truth and something indefinable that transcended both. An intrusion as crude, cruel and irrelevant as a schoolmaster's bark directed at a woolgathering pupil. *Callous, callous Ashweald, to stand there contemplating art. Art! ART!* And like a pupil in the shock of discovery and the panic of guilt, he sought respite in throwing out a truth for the wolf to devour. 'I hoped – hoped you might be willing to sell that picture . . . '

*Bloody Ashweald* . . . A man, a Russian presumably, calling him by a name he could have no reason to know . . . Speaking English . . . Bearing, beneath the Solzhenitsyn beard, a faint – no, not a *faint*, a *decided* resemblance to – to Peter! Peter! Peter Lomax Grant . . .

It must be a dream, a dream cobbled together from bits and pieces from all over time and space . . . The sort of uneasy, near-nightmare dream which at home Sue would deliver him from by throwing off the eiderdown . . . Except that he was not at home, and there was no Sue any more.

'Christ, what a laugh! You!'

Dream or no dream, only one way forward suggested itself, and he held out a hand as Stanley might have done to Livingstone. Peter, for what seemed an age, remained doubled up, indifferent to his presence. Then, slowly, he reached up and offered a hand that was dirty and bleeding.

'*You*, you're the hatchet man they've sent . . . '

'They?'

'The Firm! The bloody Firm!'

'I left it, Peter. Sue and I left it together. You were at our wedding.'

'Cover, wasn't it? Cover! I'm not taken in!'

'Cover? Playing schoolmaster for twenty bloody years! And all in aid of eventually coming to where no one knew you'd be, and where no one knows you are!'

'Where *do* they think I am?' The question flashed out like a sword.

'I've no idea. What was suggested at the time was that you'd gone to the bottom of the Solent, swimming for the mainland.'

'Me? Who hates water and can't swim a stroke!'

'I don't suppose many knew that.'

'But the Firm can't have thought I was at the bottom of the Solent. And they don't *now*, do they?'

'I've no means of knowing.'

'Easily said. Not so easily believed.'

69

'You're way out of touch, Peter.'

'Can't exactly help that, can I?'

'And not so grateful as you might be.'

'Grateful? Me? What the hell for?'

'Did none of our letters reach you?'

'Letters from you would have been surplus to entitlement. I wouldn't have seen them. They showed me birthday cards and Christmas cards – I got a lot of them.'

'Didn't counsel tell you of our offer to give evidence?'

'He may have done.'

'Christ, Peter, we did try . . . It wasn't much, but we plugged away . . . It seemed so monstrous for the press to be saying you'd done this and this – as if they'd been privy to the *in-camera* bit – when none of it coincided with what we knew of our work.'

'Well, that was nice of you. Thank you very much.' His voice was bitter. 'But why? You never struck me as Marxist-Leninists.'

'We weren't. Any more than you! The fifty-six years was what we jibbed at. They'd made a scapegoat of you. It was an obscenity of a sentence!'

'You thought they should have let me off with a caution?'

'We thought they should have sentenced you appropriately for whatever it was you pleaded guilty to. Ten or fifteen years' worth at most.'

'You did, did you? That must have endeared you to the Firm.'

'That didn't matter. What did was that MOD struck us off their free-lance translators' panel . . . '

'Not exactly a joy and comfort to my friends, was I . . . Quive-Rivers must have mentioned you, but it can't have registered . . . When you're battling not to go under in a great maelstrom of fear, self-pity, confusion and God knows what, you don't always clutch at the best of the straws . . . It all seems so long ago now, and dead . . . '

'Your attack just now seemed lively enough.'

'Blind panic . . . Blind fury . . . Vicious-dog reaction . . . Take your pick . . . '

'I came to see Leningrad, Peter, not to look for you. Some days ago I came in here and saw an artist painting. The painting's what I saw and remembered, not the artist.'

'You're not going to tell me you came here without first approaching the Firm, who said they'd be obliged if you'd keep a weather eye open . . . '

'I should have approached the Firm, I know, but I didn't. I simply came.'

Peter shook his head. 'Just how much can I believe? You're danger to me, Nick, danger and uncertainty, just when I've got used to feeling safe.'

'I intend you no harm, and shall do you no harm . . . '

'There's always the other side of the medal . . . Suppose *I* ring the *appropriate organs*, tell them we've got the master mind of *Lucky Dip* on the soil of our Soviet Motherland . . . '

'What can I tell them that you haven't already?'

'Oh, they'll think up something to pin on you, gaol you for twenty-five years, sit back and wait for an exchange offer. Sue'll raise hell to get you back, I'm certain of that.'

'Sue's dead. No one will give a bugger whether I get back or not.'

'Sue dead?' His look was both intense and puzzled. 'I'm sorry . . . Sorry . . . ' He gestured at the easel. 'You want this, you say?' There was mock incredulity in his voice. 'Do you really?'

'I do, very much.'

'It's started well – very well – but God knows how it'll finish. Look, how long have you got? When is it you leave?'

'Just over two weeks.'

'Won't be finished by then. You'll have to make another trip . . . Some time next year, say . . . But be clear about one thing, Nick: if word gets out about my being here – no painting.'

'If word gets out it won't be through me.'

71

'Are you the only one not to have gone to Tallinn?'

'Me and Lady Oakhurst.'

'Not the wife of the art historian?'

'The same.'

'Why aren't you at Tallinn? It's worth a visit.'

'I thought I'd use the time chasing the picture.'

'What brought you to the palace in the first place?'

'I was waiting for the telephone office on the Nevsky to open.'

'How come you had no lessons on a weekday morning?'

Ashweald explained.

'So I'd be safe working here till about two-thirty on a weekday?'

'I should think so.'

'Any Firm-types in your party?'

'None that I recognize.'

'Tell you what: if, by any chance, you smell danger to me, and that means to yon masterpiece – you could nip in and stick a chalk mark on the railings just here. Got any chalk? Here's a bit of yellow. That'll do. If there's no time for chalking, come in and do a clockwise round . . . Otherwise, *keep right away*. And should you see me anywhere around, *don't acknowledge me* . . . If I see chalk here, or you, I shall hop it . . . '

'How do I contact you when I come next year?'

As he'd always done at school when caught unawares, Peter tapped his forehead. 'Wait, let me think . . . Look, I wouldn't be averse to a *bit of chat*, as we used to say, if you're agreeable . . . Only not for a day or two . . . Is that a street map you've got there? Ah, dear old *Falk*! *Falk's* a king to the local product.' He took it and opened it. 'Just here, believe it or not, is a Tibetan Buddhist temple. Not many guides feature it, so it doesn't draw tourists. Come via Yelagin Island here, then by this bridge over the Bolshaya Nevka. It's no longer used as a temple, but it looks the part – truncated pyramid of dark granite, roof edges decorated in red and gold. You won't see it until you're right on top because of all the trees. Just before it there's a waste area, bit like an English car park, right down to the public bogs. OK. When you get a picture postcard at the hostel saying can't manage such and such a day, come to the temple car park at nine in the evening *on the day after the one named*. If you're prevented, come the day after that. Look for a red *Zhiguli* – yes, that one over there – parked beside the bogs. Remember all that? The Cinderella warning, though, is *make sure you're not followed*. The footbridges and long stretches of embankment will give you the means of making sure . . . But you must be off, and I must get on. Oh, I'll sign the card, er, *BG*.'

'Standing for?'

He raised a blood-smeared palm in a gesture of farewell. '*Bad Guy. Bum Geste. Ben Gunn* – whatever you like.'

Sitting with his back against a birch tree, he looked out into the Gulf of Finland. Ungainly hydrofoils plied this way and that far out in the haze, small craft motored by under taut staysail, and once a destroyer passed. The wavelets, which till then had been washing in desultory fashion over the coarse sand at the base of the red granite boulders, soon swelled to waves which darted in, shooshing like the wind through an avenue of trees, and then retreated, clattering like a Bodmin Moor brook. The sea of Cornwall would have deemed the performance unduly modest, even for a sultry day, but the small children greeted it with delight. And apart from these sights and sounds, there were scents and smells – of birchwood fires, grilling *shashlyk*; of conifers, warm grass, hot sand, brine, Balkan tobacco.

He sat, eyes half closed. The thoughts set whirling like the flakes of a snowstorm toy by his encounter with Peter had settled for the moment, but as with the toy, not much was needed to set them whirling again.

He saw himself sitting with Sue in the train to London, felt again the unusualness of it, the birth of their first child having put an end to their going everywhere together as a matter of course. They ate the sandwiches Sue had made for the journey, picturing the scene at home – Geoffrey in his high chair being fed some savoury mess. From Waterloo they walked to Lincoln's Inn, pausing in the middle of the bridge to look at the river – which after the Neva would never again seem impressive. Then, over the expanse of his desk, in something like a Cambridge college in the very heart of the City, they faced Quive-Rivers and found that there was not much they were permitted to say.

'No, I think you're right.' Pause to relight pipe with vesta. 'The provisions of the Official Secrets Act as it affects you two as individuals, clearly cannot be set aside – even in these circumstances.'

'Doesn't that rather cripple Peter's appeal from the start?' Sue asked.

Quive-Rivers shook the match out somewhere in the blue smoke. 'I would not go so far as to say that, Mrs Ashweald. Peter Grant, as you know, has pleaded guilty to a number of charges. He has already made a very full confession relating to those charges. Now, whatever you or your husband might care to tell me, if it weren't for the Act by which you are bound, it could, I imagine, only overlap the material which forms the confession . . . '

'Assuming,' Ashweald said, 'that in his confession Peter has written the truth.'

'Why should you doubt that what he has written is the truth?'

'Because I can conceive of nothing that could be done within the scope of our operations as I know them, to merit such a savage sentence.'

'Is that not simply to say that you take one view and the Chief Justice another?'

'The Chief Justice cannot know as much about Peter's work as we do. He has looked in the wrong direction and attached importance to the wrong things.'

74

'Can you be more precise?'

'Yes. *Government Official* – that was how Peter was described in court. The effect of that was to establish a convenient myth – that of the ordinary civil servant who chose to betray state secrets rather than do the decent thing – come out into the open with his new allegiance, and resign.'

'Was that then *not* the decent thing to do?'

'No,' Sue interrupted angrily. 'No, no, no. Peter wasn't a government official. He was an Intelligence agent. For the Intelligence agent, words like decency have no meaning. They don't apply. Intelligence work of our sort is quite simply *war carried on illicitly in peace*. And it's warfare far worse than the overt sort because it's totally lawless, totally unbridled – there's no Hague Convention, no sanctions against dirty tricks or dirty weapons, no code of chivalry, no Red Cross, no neutral observers! Anything goes – anything that serves the end we happen to have in mind. That kind of warfare fosters decency about as often as the wilds breed a vegetarian wolf. No, you can't expect decency, but you may find courage . . . Courage such as, rightly or wrongly, we applaud in an Igor Guzenko who comes running to us with an armful of selected secret files from his embassy cipher room. But which we do not applaud in Peter Grant when he chooses to fight on their own secret ground and by their own lawless and amoral methods, the mortal enemies of a country he prefers!'

'Are you saying, Mrs Ashweald, that such a man has no case to answer?'

'No, I am not. Of course he has a case to answer. Of course he must expect to suffer. But the punishment must fit the crime.'

'What else would you urge in support of that?'

'I would urge that a profession that sets itself above the laws of its own, or any, country – a profession which sees dishonesty and deceit as positive virtues – has no right to be unduly indignant when one of its own members resorts to treachery. Occupational diseases exist to be contracted by those who practise unhealthy occupations.'

'The topsy-turvy morality of Intelligence breeds a kind of sickness, is that it?'

'Yes,' Sue said wearily. 'That's it exactly.'

'But the plea on medical grounds is never a good batting wicket.'

'I'm not suggesting that a plea be made.'

'How do you answer the question: May not punishment of great severity deter people from giving way to illness of that sort? Illness is a thing to fight against, is it not?'

'Where faith is the illness, it is proof against all deterrents.'

'So what, ideally, do we do with Peter Grant?'

'Lock him up, say for five years until his special knowledge becomes stale, then deport him to the Soviet Union . . . For Peter to end his days there might prove a harsher punishment than any that we could devise.'

Quive-Rivers laid his pipe down beside his pouch and box of vestas; and grasping his lapels leant back and disburdened himself of an address.

'When the commando or paratrooper trained to kill in war employs that skill in peace on, shall we say, his wife's lover, he gets reminded that what he may lawfully do on behalf of his country in war, becomes a crime when he does it on his own account in war or peace. He gets that reminder, and perhaps a few years for manslaughter. With betrayal it is almost the exact reverse. No criminal penalty attaches to a man who betrays his wife because he prefers another woman. But if he betrays his country because he prefers another, he commits a crime apparently worse than murder – *four times worse* in the case of Peter Grant. The man who kills his country's enemies takes the horror of it on his own head. The soul-searchings, the sleepless nights, if any, are strictly his. Maybe that's why we're sometimes prepared to be lenient if he kills on his own account. But the man who betrays millions of his countrymen in the spirit that he might betray a wife, deserves, it seems, a punishment that reflects the harm he does to a great number, in short, to his country . . . '

Again Sue broke in angrily. 'That may be true of the man who gives away atomic secrets allegedly for the good of humanity, but it's not true of Peter. *Country* and *Intelligence department* are not the same, any more than *government official* and *Intelligence agent* are. A game played in hidden parts of a school by a handful of boys, unbeknown to their fellows, can no more be called *the school* than the rabbits on the borders of the playing fields . . . Which is why people like Peter have always to be tried *in camera* – so that no one outside the court shall ever know what vacuous, pernicious, wasteful nonsense a few overgrown schoolboys have the cheek to get up to in the country's name!'

God, if only Sue had been Peter's counsel!

The children, when called, raced happily to the shade of the birch trees for their share of the *shashlyk*. The beach was now empty . . . But no, not quite . . . To the right of his arc of vision, no great way off, a young woman not unlike Irina was sitting on a rock gazing out to sea. She was eating a *pirozhok*, holding the paper that contained it so as to stop crumbs from falling onto a green frock patterned with marigold-like blossoms. When she had finished eating, she stood up, shook out the skirt of her frock, pulled the belt straight. She was taller than Irina, slimmer, younger perhaps, but just as typically Slav. Her shoes were flat-heeled but smart, her frock was not transparent. She looked briefly in Ashweald's direction before resuming her seat and her contemplation of the sea. From time to time she lit a cigarette, and although she did not look his way again, he had the impression that she was observing him out of the corner of her eye. When he set out to catch the bus to Repino station she did not follow. At a cricket-pavilion-like structure set back from the road in an area of litter, he bought a glass of tepid and undrinkable beer and sat with it at an unwholesome rustic table. Green-dress did not pass, but a young man of semi-American appearance came and plied him with invitations to drink beer as his guest and exchange sterling for roubles, until Ashweald told him to bugger off. Green-dress reappeared on the platform at Repino, and on the crowded train to Leningrad contrived to spend the better part of an hour pressed close to him. Ashweald did not respond. He wondered what she would do when they got to Leningrad, and was not surprised when, with a toss of the head, she took the opposite direction.

# 6.

On the Sunday morning he woke to his alarm and a sense of freedom. No lectures or lessons. No conducted tours. No competition for the bathroom. No Irina to wait for. He drifted back towards sleep, and between waking and dozing experienced a moment of unusual clarity, in which questions shrilled out like a telephone in an empty house. Was Peter kept informed – perhaps by State Security – of visits by British parties, to enable him to be especially on his guard? Did he receive lists with names and photographs? Or had Peter, after spotting him, put through a call to the appropriate organs as he called them? It was hard to see otherwise how Peter could have associated him with a particular course and been aware of the trip to Tallinn. No, no more sleep! He swung himself from under the light quilt and went to fill his tin.

As he shaved, he considered the week's return on his mikes: Carvel's sexual prowess, Eleanor's snoring . . . Ought he to re-site them? Or wait another week? Re-site them where? He wetted his flannel in the tiny pool of hot water, wrung it out and pressed it to his face. In the relaxation conferred by darkness and warmth a flash of inspiration came. The telephone on the reception counter might be worth a try. Carvel and Eleanor were in the habit of using it.

The bed-sitter doors had bolts but no locks, and so it was as simple to retrieve the microphone from the back of Carvel's wardrobe as it had been to place it there. Siting it within earshot of the telephone was not going to be so simple.

The *dezhurnaya* was Tamara Vassilyevna, who now knew his name and no longer hailed him as 'young man'. He greeted her cheerily, deposited his key, took a copy of *Leningradskaya Pravda* over to one of the easy chairs with which the vestibule was furnished, and consulted the tiny cinema column.

Heavens, the camera! Why, how, had he never noticed it, placed to secure a full face picture of anyone approaching the counter from the door? Now there ought also to be – and from the corner of his eye he saw that there was – another camera to catch the profile. Why cameras? Not for the course members – they'd supplied photographs with their visa applications. Perhaps, then, for the identification of visitors . . . He replaced the paper and made towards the phone. 'Tamara Vassilyevna, it is possible, I take it, to ring England from here. . .'

'Possible, Nikolay Karlovich, but not until after ten. Then it will be a question of ordering the call and waiting perhaps an hour for the connection. A more convenient possibility is the International Post Office, 6, Nevsky Prospekt – except that today is their exit day. And there is the Long-Distance Telephone Exchange in Herzen Street . . . '

'Can you tell me what the procedure is at the Herzen Street Exchange?' His exploring fingers encountered a groove on the underside of the counter overhang against which he was leaning. The groove led to a drilled hole which seemed ideal. Into it he slipped the tiny, self-adhering radio microphone he had been holding in his hand. Whether he would ever be able to retrieve it remained to be seen.

The *Visla* was uncrowded enough for him to secure his favourite seat by the window with the rubber plant and the voluminous net curtain. As he ate his black bread and drank his black coffee, his eye followed the elegant embankment railings: away from the window, then sharp left to escort Red Bridge across the Moyka, then sharp left again to line the far embankment, where their simple pattern – though reduced in size – stood out boldly against the sun-brilliant house fronts. As in his beloved courtyard and most other parts of the city, the rigidity of the wrought iron and the severe symmetry and bulk of embankment and building were offset by the mobile, almost ethereal beauty of foliage. There was also the quiver of reflected water, the one element which the courtyard lacked. It was a commonplace enough view, but one which cheered and encouraged him immeasurably, although he could not have said why. A view which, like the city itself, seemed to radiate a contented, optimistic quality infinitely greater than the sum of its parts. Oh, to be here in innocence, unburdened by a vague but insistent sense of mission, and of guilt at being so lukewarm in its execution!

Espionage, he had read, is a life-or-death game of chess against oneself as well as one's opponent. Sitting here, in the *Visla*, in Leningrad, over an unaccustomed second cup of coffee, he saw the truth of the adage, saw too, how cheerfulness and optimism might crumble away like sandcastles before the tide.

Who, *who* could Archie's target be? If Peter, what had prevented his saying so from the start? What could be the point of sending an agent in a state of total ignorance to discharge a nameless mission? To play sitting duck? Like the woman in the green dress? A Heath-Robinsonish cross between trout-fly and lightning conductor?

'*Vy razreshayete* – You permit?' An effeminate young man in natty suit, shirt, tie, was motioning with his head at the empty place opposite Ashweald.

'*Pozhaluysta.*'

If Archie *did* have some target for him as missile, some purpose other than his own destruction, then he *must* somehow somewhere have built in *something* to point him in the right direction.

Carvel and Eleanor – they had been built in . . . *Should be more worth watching than the rest* . . . Carvel and Eleanor. In bloody Tallinn. With Irina. While he sat in Leningrad, with a long-forgotten spy and dreams of a picture . . .

Draining his coffee, he became aware that the young man opposite, as he chewed, kept looking up at him. The man's face was powdered, his eyes clumsily made up. The girl in green had worn no make-up at all . . . He returned his cup and plate to the counter, saluted the buxom blonde, thanked her for her advice to go to the sea, and made for the door. The young man was reaching across the table for a square of paper, and his jacket had ridden up to reveal part of a squat brown holster.

Ashweald set off along Dzerzhinsky Street at a cracking pace. Just short of the Plekhanov Street junction he slowed to watch women mixing cement to be hodded, with loads of brick, by other women up four floors of scaffolding to where yet other women were repairing the wall. A glance showed the street behind to be empty.

The Tikhvin Cemetery was shut. No one knew when it would be open. It might, an old man volunteered, even be under repair. Ashweald smiled inwardly. Repair of the mausoleum on Red Square had resulted in the removal of Stalin's body from beside Lenin's. He walked on. The path, becoming suddenly like a drawbridge, led over a moat-like little river towards the gateway of the Alexander Nevsky Monastery. Again, a Cambridge-college atmosphere concocted out of non-Cambridge ingredients – baroque buildings, terracotta relieved by white, classical cathedral in place of chapel, trees full of cawing rooks . . . Old women were begging, and one was being taken to task by a man of middle-class attire but with coarse peasant features. Ashweald caught the words *blemish on the healthy features of Soviet society* . . . Would that be Ernie's view also? Like the gypsies in Gorky Gardens, the old women did not look starved or downtrodden. And yet they were begging . . .

The cathedral was crowded with men and women, young

82

and old. The air, heavy with incense, now was set throbbing by the rich bass of an officiant, now was sent rippling this way and that like a cornfield before the breeze, as many voices responded from the choir loft. Up, up into the lofty dome the Old Church Slavonic words went sailing, nasals and all, up into the dome to be lost like widening circles on the surface of a lake, or perhaps, in some mysterious way, to be preserved there. He moved this way and that between the standing worshippers, watched the veneration of icons and of the shrine where the remains of St Alexander Nevsky once reposed. The singing, the harmony of the building, the rapt devotion held him in thrall. He began a prayer, but words, thoughts dissolved instantly in pure emotion.

He came out into blinding light, fresh air and the racket of rooks, and felt as if he had narrowly escaped suffocation. Was this the Church Dostoyevsky had known? Had it been thus on the day of his funeral? Gold glittered, candle-eyes shone bright in the gloom, the sun shafted down through billowing incense smoke and the ascending human voices as always, but they combined now to create an all-pervading, all-inhibiting, near-electric emotional charge, not faith, not love of God, but a thing in itself . . .

The simplicity of the Anichkov Bridge over the Fontanka, the absolute rightness of the rearing-horse-with-trainer statues at its approaches, the perfect proportions and absolute symmetry of the Palace of Young Pioneers dragged him back into the here and now. This city and its astonishing beauty, created at the cost of vast human suffering, destroyed at the cost of vast human suffering, and restored at the cost of unimaginable self-sacrifice, had become in themselves a force for good, a source of inspiration and strength and courage. A cross of suffering, but as such, a symbol with a message of hope. Turgenev found it impossible to believe that *such a language as ours should not have been given to a great people*. No less true was that a people that kept faith by its monuments must also be great. In England the inspiring beauty of garden and building was largely private; here, the beauty of both was entirely public, a thing to be shared, to offset the shortcomings of the private . . .

He had, without noticing, taken a side turning off the Nevsky and was now confronting an elegantly collonaded building. For a moment he stood savouring the words *Saltykov-Shchedrin State Public Library*, then, struck by sudden inspiration, entered.

In the cool, ancestral mansion atmosphere of the interior, he was passed from check-desk to check-desk with a style of gesture that was pure Whitehall, until at last he reached a formidable white-haired matron who required the filling in of a questionnaire concerning academic qualifications and area of research. This done, he was motioned to an alcove well-stocked with elevating reading matter, and after some ten minutes was called back to the table. Handing him his reader's card, the formidable matron wore an expression midway between the fatuous purposefulness of a headmaster bestowing colours and the triumph of a conjuror producing a rabbit.

Thence to the gentlemen's cloakroom whose door proved difficult to open. Once inside, he saw why. Scholarly men, all smoking their heads off, were performing the difficult feat of feigning indifference to each other's presence while enjoying the elbow room of tinned sardines. Getting to where he wanted and back was like rowing a dinghy against tide and wind. Every breath he took was like inhaling a whole cigar.

The main index was open to the public, the shelves were not. If the titles he wanted were in the library, he would have to fill in a requisition form, and that would provide a pointer to his line of interest: *Vanishing Trick* by Jim Pearl, the cockney mail-train robbery genius, who claimed to have sprung Peter from Parkhurst by the complicated method described; and *Lone Battle*, Peter's somewhat sketchy autobiography highlighting his years with the Firm, for five of which he had been in the employ of its rival, the KGB.

With *Pearl*, however transliterated, he drew a blank, but *Grant* was there, not in English or in Russian but in an East German edition entitled *Im Einsatz fürs sozialistische Mutterland*. Heaven be praised! A vestige of cover! Put down in the questionnaire as a student of Russian and German life and letters, he could now choose half a dozen other high-sounding titles from *GDR*, *Political* and requisition them together. The librarian quickly produced all seven volumes, and he made his way to an empty table in a spacious reading-room.

*Lone Battle* had been published in 1974, the year after *Vanishing Trick*, and some five years after the extraordinary admission that Peter had 'disappeared' from prison. On each occasion Sue had ordered a copy from their local bookseller, and as soon as it turned up, they sat side by side, washing-up, children, even dog, forgotten, and read avidly, as they might a letter from a friend who had long not written. But the man described in the one, and named as author of the second, was not recognizably the Peter Grant they'd known. *Vanishing Trick* was no more than a fictional cash-in on a clever idea. *Lone Battle* must have been ghosted for the greater glory of the Firm in the service of some inscrutable purpose. No less incredible than the Peter who was not Peter, was the work that Peter claimed to have been employed on. A little was like the real thing, but most was a curious cocktail: one part Maugham, one part Greene, one part le Carré, shaken not stirred, and garnished with blarney. And each time, when the incredulity and puzzlement had worn off, they'd consigned the book to an inconspicuous shelf and let Peter slip gradually out of mind again.

The closing sentences of *Lone Battle* were memorably lame, the sort of thing an indifferent pupil rounds off an essay with to be in time for the match on tele. Turning to the final page of *Im Einsatz fürs sozialistische Mutterland*, he saw that the translator had done a faithful job.

*Another Christmas – my fifth . . . I had by now served what I deemed a reasonable term. Next year, I resolved, I would leave prison and return to life. And as the world knows, I did.*

Ashweald went back to page one.

*I was born in a house overlooking St Ives Bay in Cornwall and the lighthouse which Virginia Woolf celebrates in the novel of that name. My bedroom window had just that view, and as soon as I was able, I would push a chair to the window, climb on it and look out at the bay and the white wall surrounding the white lighthouse on its dark island. I watched the changing sea and the changing sky, and my bear watched with me, and we were happy. It was quite a while before I shifted my gaze in to the window world of myself and my bear, and when I did, I saw that the varnish on the plain wood window ledge was boiling into little bubbles in the heat of the sun. The bubbling of that varnish in the sun, roughening the smooth clean surface and muddying the bold sweeps and whorls of the grain, was, I am sure, the cause of the first deep dissatisfaction I ever felt. It now seems symbolic that my first dissatisfaction should have been an environmental one. And so, in origin at least, was my second.*

*The bear was soon replaced in my affections by a fine Cairn terrier, Humphrey, and in no time I was old enough to walk him on my own, which I did at all times of the day, but never with keener enjoyment than in the hour before breakfast. What I enjoyed were the scents of sea and sand, of sand and grass, and grass and sea – not the effete grass of lawn and bowling green, but coarse, robust grass of dune and towan, grass which, bent by the breeze or wind, would describe arcs in the moist sand, sometimes near-perfect circles. Humphrey took pleasure in the scents, but more especially he liked charging great distances at knots of seagulls who, at the very last minute, would take to the air leaving him looking foolish and lonely.*

*There was a river, blood-red from tin, which ran out through red sand to the sea and stained the sea far out, as could be seen from the cliff top. There were remnants of heaven knows what installations, a dead city now – or so we imagined it, Humphrey and I, wandering its ins and outs in awed silence. Later there came a time when such remnants and ruins of past industries seemed blots on the landscape less monstrous but no whit less offensive than the white pyramids or sky dumps thrown up by china clay quarriers. Later still, at Cambridge, when I became more conscious politically and economically, I saw that the decline of the tin and china clay industries involved considerations over and above aversion to the ugliness of their debris . . .*

No, this wasn't Peter. Memories, such as those of Gwithian, had some root in reality, were recognizable foundation stones. But the edifices built upon and around them were wildly improbable – the social and political conscience whose Cambridge stirrings had their origin in Gwithian, for example. Peter had had no stirrings of social or political conscience at Cambridge. Nor had Archie. Nor had Ashweald. At the Cambridge of the late forties it was no longer the rule for clever but callow minds to embrace Russian communism as the cure for man's ills. Clever, callow, they may have been, he, Archie and Peter, but never so naive, self-righteous, over-credulous and downright bloody silly as that!

Peter's ghost-writer plonked him fairly and squarely in the Great Tradition of British espionage. He – or she – adhered firmly to that naive, self-righteous, over-credulous and downright bloody silly school of journalism that pretends to analyse and explain treachery. And does so, oblivious to the fact that there must, as Anna Karenina said of *kinds of love*, be just as many kinds of treachery as there are heads, minds and hearts – if by treachery is meant doing the reverse of what the state feels entitled to expect.

That was one thing. Quite another was the cold-bloodedness of one particular incident. Reading it for the first time, years before, he had discounted it as part and parcel of the general fiction. Now, re-reading it, he sensed an underlying reality, a reality which resided if not in the incident itself, then in the purpose of portraying the incident at all. It was the point at which either Peter chose to alienate sympathy from himself completely, or the ghost-writer chose to alienate sympathy from Peter. The probability seemed in favour of the latter.

*It was a Monday morning. I had got to the office a bit on the late side, and was well infected with a sense of guilt even before Anne, my PA, greeted me with 'D's been buzzing you non-stop since nine bloody fifty!'*

*I checked my appearance in Anne's mirror, picked up half a dozen files at random to give myself a busy air, and tootled along to the Director's sanctum.*

*D's PA was literally bouncing on her tailor-made swivel-chair. 'You must, absolutely must, Peter, always leave your whereabouts with Anne. Go in, don't stay to knock for pity's sake!'*

*The Old Man was pacing, intent on a sheaf of flimsies, signals from Eurostations, all hot from the deciphering machines. Seeing me, he flipped back to page one, which was pink. Pink denotes a signal transmitted out of schedule by non-interceptable method reserved for emergency or trouble.*

*'Take a pew,' the Old Man said. 'Read that.'*

*The flimsy read:* = TOP SECRET = URGENT = DIRINT PERSONAL = FROM 309 HEADINT = PER XTX = BEGIN = EIGHT SIX ONE REPORTS SECRET UNOFF DISCUSSIONS WITH NINE ONE RPT NINE ONE SIC RPT SIC = EIGHT SIX ONE CONVINCED SINCERITY = WISH DEFECT UK LONG CONSIDERED = STIPULATES COMMUNI-

CATE THIS TO YOU NOT BY RADIO OR NB RPT NB DIPBAG BUT SEND YOU COURIER TO REPORT WISH AS ABOVE AND OBTAIN AGREEMENT GRANT ASYLUM AND ESTABLISH TIME AND ORGANIZATION OF DEFECTION = WE SHORTHANDED HENCE PRESENT XTX = NINE ONE REQUIRES REPLY ON THESE THREE POINTS AT MEETING WITH EIGHT SIX ONE TOMORROW 640914 AT 2000 GMT = NINE ONE ALSO REQUIRES YOU TO INFORM ZERO ZERO EIGHT RPT ZERO ZERO EIGHT OF TIMINGS TO ENABLE HIM TO TAKE PROTECTIVE ACTION = THIS LAST VITAL = ADVISE US ETA OF YOUR OFFICER WITH REPLIES AND POWER TO SUPERVISE AS NECESSARY = MUST ATTEND HERE FOR BRIEFING BY 1430 GMT 640914 = END = 309 HEADINT =

*I may say that as I read the signal my bowels turned to ice, and they remained so as I handed it back with – I hoped – a nonchalant '309, that's Don, Vienna Station, isn't it?'*

*'Aye. It is. And nine one, believe it or not, Peter my lad, is their Ambassador himself, Komarov, P.P.'*

*I whistled incredulity in the approved manner. 'That explains the* sic, *then.'*

*'That explains the* sic, *Peter, as you say. But what troubles me is the dipbag reference. Doesn't it you?'*

*I played slow witted, said it seemed superfluous, there being hardly time to use the bag anyway.*

*The Old Man pulled a long face and stroked the point of his chin as a sheikh might his beard. 'I don't think it means* our *bag. My very nasty idea is that friend Komarov is tipping the wink to those of us in the know that he's got an angle on our dipbag operation . . . I hope I'm wrong for all our sakes, but the sooner he joins us, the sooner we'll know. Which brings me to business. Anne's got you on the 1350 from Gatwick, and she's laid on a car.*

'As to Komarov, he's to be told that he and his family –
there's a child or children, I think – anyway, he and his can
count on asylum, provided he's not fleeing criminal charges
. . . The usual guff.

'Direct contact with Komarov you leave entirely to 861. 861
will tell you how Komarov proposes to play it. You take over
from there, organize the safest continuation possible. But move
bloody fast, because once they get wind, they'll knock him off,
together with his wife, children and dachshund, if any. I'll get
plain-clothes SAS in from British Forces Germany. They'll be
at your disposal. Weston and Knowles will be on your flight
travelling as Queen's Messengers. They'll be carting handguns
and ammo for the SAS. They'll be at your disposal too. Don
knows our safe houses in Germany if you decide to go for an
RAF plane. And Don will finance you.

'Off you go, then. And remember, there must be no cock
up . . .'

I took another look at the signal. The 008 troubled me. I
asked casually who that was.

'You worry about Komarov, Peter. Leave this end to me.'

I walked down to the car in a daze. Komarov was going to
do for me unless I could do for him first. What Moscow had
learnt from me of the Firm's ability to read part of one dipbag
in twenty on the Vienna–Moscow run, Moscow must have
conveyed to Komarov. It was the very worst sort of short-
circuit the agent has to fear. The likelihood was that the date on
which Komarov received the tip-off not to entrust certain
matters to the bag would coincide with the date of my own
indoctrination into the operation. D would be sure to register
this in his dispassionate way, and on the quiet, just as a precau-
tion, would have me very thoroughly taken to bits and
inspected. It was me or Komarov. And time was not on my
side.

I got the driver to go via my flat so that I could pick up my
passport. This was the moment to use my last-resort one-time-
only emergency procedure. Dial a number, wait for the receiver

*to be lifted, ring off. Count twenty, dial again, allow one ring, then ring off. Then, on the underside of a small packet of tissues in the bathroom I wrote in invisible ink:* Urgent: Ambassador Komarov Vienna about to defect to British decisive rendezvous 640914 at 2000 GMT where not known Rockefeller.

*They had a key to my flat. They would send a girl, the kind it's no surprise to see slipping into or out of a young man's flat. Into her handbag would go the box of tissues. Down the drain would go Komarov.*

*Mind easier, heart pounding, I rushed down the stairs two at a time. I'd remembered my passport. Remembered to flush the invisible ink out of the fountain pen and fill with real ink. A few days in Vienna would make a nice break. In four or five hours I'd be sitting in a restaurant garden under the chestnuts over a litre jug of Gösser and* The Times *crossword. There'd be trout. A mushroom omelette with salad would do if there wasn't . . .*

Peter did a lot of sitting about in restaurant gardens. 861 did not return from his rendezvous with Komarov. Komarov and his wife were flown to the Soviet Union for surgery following a motor smash.

At Gatwick, Weston and Knowles said there would be a car waiting. It proved to be a Jaguar of the latest model. Peter was looking forward to riding back to the office in it. Someone got out. It was not the driver to open the door, but Detective Chief Superintendent Murchison of Special Branch to take him into custody on a number of charges.

Like a stuck examinee, Ashweald gazed unseeingly at the rows of tables in front of him. The signal had a surprising ring of truth about it. So, come to that, did D's evasion over the double-zero cover number. But the emergency procedure was nonsense, pure invention. No Soviet-trained control would make so elementary and suicidal a blunder as to require his agent to ring a probably suspect, probably tapped number as summons to a pick-up at the *agent's own address*!

The mention of Don – Don Warburton – was surprising, being the only name, apart from Peter's, he recognized as real. Also real was *Lucky Dip*, the diplomatic bag tap, an operation which Ashweald had himself pioneered and then directed. It was an intricate but unusually detection-proof operation, its sheer preposterousness serving as its best camouflage. *The enemy would need to be told it was happening in order to know that it was* was the phrase he had used in his application to D for permission. That the enemy might indeed be told – by Peter! – had never crossed his mind.

He returned to the book. He was about half-way through. The trial was disposed of in less than a page, the rest was a detailed account of Peter's life in prison. This, at his first reading, Ashweald had flicked through in search of details of the escape, and finding none, had taken Rob for an overdue walk, leaving Sue to read on. Now, lunch and hunger forgotten, it was he who read on, reminded again and again how Sue had been moved to tears, and now understanding why. Like *The Ballad of Reading Gaol* she'd said . . . It seemed as if Peter's ghost-writer, not seeing how to twist the source at this point, had not bothered to try.

Peter told of his struggles, feeble at first, then gradually more assured, against the torments of solitude; of his joy at rediscovering and practising, in the mind's eye, a boyhood facility for shaping the world on paper and canvas; of the ecstasy of being at last allowed paper and water-colours, then canvas and oils; of his obsession to capture the exercise-yard in all its moods. This Peter may not have been the man he had known, but he was a credible extension of him.

It was getting on for five when Ashweald turned the last page. The concluding sentences read like the ghost's one contribution to the second part. Gathering together his books, he stiffly made his way to return them.

Outside, the sun blazed and blinded, the air clung like warm treacle. The walk to the hostel was a feat of endurance, like plodding across the Sahara or the Empty Quarter. He was glad to reach his room and throw himself on his bed.

When he awoke, the sun was gone, and a breeze was blowing the net curtains into the room. No sign of Carvel. The water – wonder of wonders! – the water was hot. He took a bath, did some washing, changed into cool things and sat on his bed to read. He opened a can of Lager, then at random, *Eugene Onegin*, and read, in Russian:

> *A moment back, that heart was beating*
> *with fire, with hate, with hope, with love,*
> *life sported there, the blood was busy;*
> *but now, as with an empty dwelling,*
> *all inside is hushed and dark;*
> *a silence has come down forever;*
> *shut are the shutters, windows whited.*
> *Gone is the owner of the place –*
> *and God knows where – he's left no trace!*

The death of Lensky, the death of the Komarovs, of Sue, of anybody – the manner of dispatch might be different, but the emptiness, the emptiness left behind was always the same.

The outer door was opening. It must be Carvel. His own door was opening. It was Irina. He rose to his feet. Irina hesitated, then threw her arms about his neck. He held her close, his face in her fragrant hair.

'Oh, Nicholas, how I missed you!'

Irina had come on alone. The others, *guts rattling*, as Ernie put it, had gone for a meal. Ashweald boiled eggs, cut bread, made coffee. After, they went for a walk in the cool evening. Hand in hand they walked, and in silence, to the Square of Arts, and in the little area of flower beds and trees, sat on a bench and looked up at Pushkin on his plinth. Soon after eleven, still hand in hand, they returned to the hostel. In the corridor, midway between their rooms, they stood facing each other, holding hands, leaning back, as if about to form a bridge for Oranges and Lemons.

'You'll wait for me for breakfast?'

'Of course.'

'Goodnight, Nicholas.'

'Goodnight, Irina.'

He had held her, fed her; they had walked hand in hand, sat with their arms about each other's waist; they had spoken hardly at all. He had wanted to kiss her, make love, but he had done neither. Something was wrong. She was, he guessed, in a state not unlike that of shock.

'How was Tallinn?' he called to Carvel through the open door.

'You should have come. Bags of scope for your German.'

'Any extraordinary occurrences, as the phrase is?'

'Absolutely none. Went like clockwork.'

'How was Irina?'

'Quiet. Probably missing you.'

'Where did you go for your meal?'

'*Pribaltiyskaya*. You should give it a try. But come and have a Lager . . . '

# 7.

From Carvel he learnt nothing to account for a state of shock on Irina's part. The following day she was early for their breakfast rendezvous – so early that they saw the buff-coloured *Zhiguli* draw up at the kerb and the driver perform the ritual of removing removable fittings. The female bricklayers were taking turns at cranking the cement mixer, and Irina and Ashweald were practically at the *Visla* by the time it chugged into life.

'Travelling companions agreeable?' he asked after her account of the trip.

'Very. You know, Ernie, for all his aggressiveness – '

'For all his north countryness, you mean . . . '

'Is that what it is?' Her surprise struck him as odd. 'Well, despite his whatever-it-is, Ernie's rather nice. Tolerant, sensitive, considerate. You get a wrong view of people because so often what you build on is a first impression, not the real them. I've seen Ernie differently since Tallinn. Thanks to Eleanor. She let fly at him in a horrible, bitchy sort of way. I'd have let fly back, but Ernie stayed perfectly calm and Christian – like, like Father Zosima!'

To Ashweald who saw Ernie more as Friar Tuck than as Dostoyevsky's soldier-turned-saint, the simile came as a shock. 'Let fly? What about?'

'It was a hangover speaking, I think. She'd drunk most of a bottle of whisky the night before. We were in that half-in-half-out-of-the-couchette state waiting and waiting for the train to stop. Ernie was half way down the corridor with our

95

cases. *And so we say hello to a new republic!* he said in a twangy American voice to no one in particular. A sort of meaningless catch-phrase, but it set Eleanor going. *Republic be buggered . . . Soviet doormat . . .* On and on, like a tutor demolishing an essay. Ernie seemed not to notice – he couldn't turn round with the cases anyway – and that enraged her. All he did say – and very quietly, as if to her alone – was *Oh, keep it for your fascist rag, lass . . .!* Which shut her up. Is she a journalist? I thought she was a don.'

'Maybe she's both.'

'Which paper is a fascist rag?'

'I'm not sure,' he said untruthfully.

'Oh, and something that would have made you laugh. For the rest of Saturday Ernie was the model tourist, hanging on the guide's every word, feeding the questions guides like to answer: total number of cobblestones in the square; how far, laid end to end, the alleys of Tallinn would stretch . . . '

'All in his fluent Russian?'

'No, they gave us English-speaking guides – I think because they're not all that keen on Russian. It certainly suited Ernie. He was affability itself. Hardly a word about lavatories or the state of his insides. Then on Sunday, after breakfast, just as we were boarding the inevitable coach, who do we see but Ernie in company with a most attractive brunette heading for what people said was a Mercedes. The next we saw of them was a few minutes before our train was due to leave, when they came tripping along the platform arm in arm, chatting away in God knows what language. Eleanor stuck her vanity mirror out of the ventilator window to watch them say goodbye and gave a running commentary . . . *He's kissing her, lifting her feet clear off the ground . . .* When he joined us in our compartment, Eleanor asked him if he'd had a good day, but all he'd say was *Middling, Eleanor, thank you. Middling.*'

'But they were friends again?'

'They were friends again soon after the outburst. She's like that.'

'What do you make of her?'

'I don't know.' Her tone suggested that she did, but wasn't going to say, so that he was surprised when she added 'What I don't like is how, when she's paralytically drunk, she suddenly fires off a question better not asked.'

'Such as?'

'Oh, it doesn't matter.'

'Your Nicholas, Irina, how does he make out in bed?' suggested itself as a possibility, and he let the question drop. At that very moment, through some trick of light and positioning, framed by the window with its view, through the net curtain, of Red Bridge, Irina took on a startlingly icon-like appearance. That of an ultra-modern icon . . . *Irina of Leningrad* . . . If only he could possess Peter's skill, just long enough to record her then and there . . .

'Come on, cheer up, Nicholas . . .' She laid a hand over his on the table. 'No lessons, remember? We're going to Petrodvoryets. Let's go and see if we can find something to buy for our picnic.'

'Yes, let's.'

Only now did he notice the shadows beneath her eyes, the tenseness in her face, and realize that her reason for being early was simply that she hadn't slept.

' . . . There we see the Grand Cascade. It comprises three çascades, sixty-four fountains and thirty-seven statues. Best known of the statues, and centre piece, is the gilt Samson Fountain showing Samson rending the jaws of the lion. And as we can see, from the foot of the Grand Cascade, between fountains and ultimately into the Gulf of Finland, runs a canal. This is called the Sea Canal . . . '

They were standing on the terrace of the severely plain but engagingly handsome Grand Palace waiting their turn to go in, and the guide was tuning up her voice for the great series of cadenzas it was shortly to embark upon. Ashweald felt again the irritation and guilt he had suffered as a child at never managing to enter into the spirit of rapt reverence exhibited by the rest of the congregation. Irina, Carvel, Eleanor, Ernie were managing to be raptly reverent. What prevented him from being the same?

In a little while – when the guide had finished with the statues, all as fussily vulgar, against the studied reticence of the yellow and white palace, as a string of china geese against a plaster wall – in a little while, they would be led in through one of the doors, they would drag elasticated felt *tapochki* over their shoes to protect the parquet, and go padding off past evil-smelling cloakrooms to the foot of yet another of Russia's myriad highly-ornate grand staircases. Guiding would then commence in earnest, and as the morning wore on, the Ancient Mariner would begin to seem downright taciturn. The sheer number of remarkable things to see, the sheer number of remarkable facts to be communicated – *they* were the trouble, being infinitely more than flesh and blood could absorb at a sitting – a hundredweight of chocolates instead of a box, a gallon of whisky instead of a double . . .

As one exquisitely conceived, decorated and furnished room opened into another, the only relief was to stand by a window and drink in the beauty of a tree against sea or sky or ornamental garden. That little at least could be savoured . . .

From the mighty proportions, diamond sparkle and arresting white of the Throne Room, they passed into the smaller Chesma Hall, where the white of walls and ceiling was covered with canvases.

'Pleasure,' Carvel said out of the corner of his mouth, 'is doing what you don't tire of; interest is not tiring of what you are doing; and doing what you *are* tired of doing, is endurance; but . . . '

But the eye of the guide was upon them, and she waited until sure of their attention before continuing, 'The canvases are by Hackert. They represent, first . . . '

Quietly, so as not to give others the same idea, Ashweald told Carvel, when the time came to go, that he and Irina would prefer to stay on at Petrodvoryets and make their own way back.

'Sound idea,' Carvel responded. 'Great relief to follow your noses for a bit, instead of marching with a group.'

So they followed their noses to *Mon Plaisir*, the smaller palace set at the very edge of the sea where, earlier, they had eaten their picnic lunch, and sat again before the same balustrade and the same glassy Gulf.

He rummaged in his briefcase. 'Not much left to eat.'

'I don't care. If I'm to die of hunger, let it be with you, and here.'

A silence as mighty and commanding as the flaming gold of the sinking sun lay upon the water, from which rounded rocks protruded like the rumps of hippopotami.

'Nicholas,' she said, then after a silence, 'that night we went to the restaurant, you asked me something which I avoided answering because I didn't want to lie . . . I said yes, it was my first visit to Leningrad. And that was true. This is my first visit, in the strict sense – *my first since leaving* . . . No, don't say anything, Nicholas, please.' She put a hand to his arm. 'Don't say anything . . . Let me tell you what I want to tell you – what I wanted to tell you this morning when you were looking out of the window, at the house I used to live in . . .

'I was born here in Leningrad. Like my parents before me. I'm more Russian than Tatiana – something I think she's suspected from the first, just as you did, for a moment, at Pulkovo.

'It's almost the anniversary of the day I left, the fifteenth. It was my birthday. I was ten. My grandparents drove me to Pulkovo in their car. I was to fly to Moscow alone and be met by a Foreign Ministry official who would put me onto the plane for London. Oh, I was so sad at leaving. I didn't want to go. No, no, no. I wish now I'd run away and hidden. I took my Mishka to say goodbye to my dear, dear Moyka. I sat him on the railing – it's just the same as it was then, smooth, like a key that's been used for countless years. I must have looked across to the *Visla*, where we go so often, and the Chemical Cleaners a door or two away, but I can't have seen them through my tears.

'In Moscow they showed me Red Square, the Kremlin, *Children's World*. They wouldn't believe that I didn't want anything bought for me in *Children's World*. They took me on the river, and I thought how inferior it was to the Neva. Inferior, like everything else in Moscow. They gave me a lavish meal. I began to realize by then that my father must be important. They gave me flowers for the plane, and chocolates.

'My mother was at London Airport to meet me. In English clothes. I hardly knew her. She had a car waiting, more impressive than grandpa's car, and she got into the driving seat and drove. I never knew before that she could. We went to Highgate, where we had a house of three floors all to ourselves, and a garden with trees and flowers and grass. I began to cheer up, just a little.

'We lived almost next door to the Cooks. Dr Cook, Gerald, had lived with us for a year when I was small. My father was Professor of Physics at the university then, and Dr Cook and he had some speciality in common. I remember him, when I was small, saying *How do you do* to Mishka. And I remember howling because I didn't like the sound of the English words. Now I had a chance to speak the English I had learnt at school. I got on well with Barbara Cook who was exactly my age. My parents said I must learn all the English I could. It would help my studies, and later on it would help my career. In September I went to school – not to the embassy school with other Soviet children, but where Barbara went, a private day school for girls. I had to wear a blazer and a straw boater, play hockey, learn judo . . .

'My parents continued to travel a great deal, and as if to

make up for the time I spent with the Cooks as one of their family, every Sunday morning I had to go to an off-shoot of the embassy near us in Highgate. There I spent from nine till two with a tutor: four hours of instruction, then, over lunch, an hour spent detailing all that I had done at school during the week, which wasn't easy because I hadn't always got the Russian words for what I wanted to explain. But I enjoyed my sessions with Larisa Ivanovna. The worst part was not being able to eat as much as I wanted, because of having to talk.

'What I especially looked forward to were the pictures in the room where I had lessons. They were all of Leningrad, nothing special, just coloured photographs, but they were home. Real home. Sometimes, when she was in a good mood, Larisa Ivanovna would shut her book, sit back, point at a picture and say, *Irina Pavlovna, imagine yourself in that picture, right there, back to the Alexander Column and facing towards the Winter Palace. Now describe the way from there to your home.* Tears would come into her eyes as well as mine. She was a Leningrader and as homesick as I was.

'Then a time came when I lived with the Cooks for a whole year, and Larisa Ivanovna questioned me closely about life with them. I say a year, but it was really just the thirty school weeks. In the holidays I went to Vienna. My father was serving temporarily as ambassador there. Barbara came too. We loved Vienna, and I felt more at home there than in London. Barbara was good at German, which was a help in getting around, as I knew none.

'It was summer when I was last there, terribly hot, just as it's been today. My father's replacement had arrived. Father was in process of handing over to him, and he expected that he and mother would be back in Highgate before the end of September. They saw Barbara and me off at Schwechat on the 12th, because we were due to begin school on the 14th. I was excited and happy. By the time the excitement of the first fortnight had worn off, we'd all be together again.

'Starting school no longer held any terrors. I knew about

101

moving to new lockers, stowing shoe-bags, sports gear and all the rest, and I wasn't an outsider to the excited jabbering any more, but part of it. After which came the calm, the freshness of the first lesson, which was French. I was feeling so, so happy. Then the headmistress put her head round the door. *Miss Hetherington, I'd like Irina and Barbara to come with me, if you please* . . . I tried hard to think of something I'd done wrong – of something we'd both done wrong . . .

'It was Alma – Mrs Cook – who was waiting in the headmistress's study, and I couldn't think why, since it was less than a hour since she had dropped us both with our kit. She wasn't her usual assured, soignée self. She was dishevelled, strained, tense-looking . . . Gerald, she said, had received a message from my father. Because of certain sudden political difficulties, I must, for safety's sake, leave London at once. He and Mummy would be joining me sooner than expected. He'd explain then. Meanwhile we must keep clear of London for a time. I asked if there was going to be a war. Alma smiled a weary washed-out smile and said no, of course not.

'She had Gerald's big car instead of the family estate she'd brought us to school in. No sooner were we roaring away than I remembered Mishka. He must be got away for safety's sake too. Alma said no, he'd be all right where he was, keeping an eye on my room, but I held out. If Mishka wasn't coming, neither was I. She got me to tell her exactly where he was, then stopped at a kiosk to telephone. No need to worry. He'd be with us by evening, she said. That was a promise.

'We left London in a direction I'd never been in before – over Westminster Bridge, then south. Barbara said we must be going to the Isle of Wight and got more and more excited. Alma said we might be, she'd have to see . . . The speedometer needle was right down by the hundred mark. I thought at first it must have fallen off.

'The sea was like oil, as we crossed to the island on the ferry – just as it is out there. A golden autumn sun beat down through the mist. Big boats shot out at us suddenly and vanished again. Where we landed the air was full of shrieking gulls. It was like being on holiday all over again, except that we were still in school tunics, shirts and ties . . .

'Mishka did come that evening, but my parents didn't. Mishka came with Gerald and a man from Vienna with a ridiculously big moustache . . . '

Ashweald sat pale and aghast. It was unbelievable – the dreaded nightmare of childhood, updated, adapted, redesigned for adulthood! The same paralysing horror and foreboding mingled with the same dogged, unreasoning, nonsensical hoping for the best . . .

' . . . Between them they broke it to me: motor accident. Mummy, Daddy, both killed instantly . . .

'I was too numbed, too overwhelmed at first to be unhappy. Unhappiness came as it sank in that those waves and smiles and blown kisses at Schwechat were the end . . . Mishka and I were alone . . .

'In time I thought of my grandparents. Wouldn't they be wanting me to go back? I asked. That, I can see now, was the hardest of the questions Alma and Gerald had to answer.

'Breaking it to a child that mother and father are dead is bad enough, but it can be done, for the child knows its loss. What the child doesn't know, and can't know, is what espionage is, or treachery. And the child can't be told what they are, any more than a man blind from birth can be told the colour of milk. *Dead* was how they chose to put it. You can't tell a puffy-eyed little girl with pigtails clutching a teddy bear that dead means as good as dead. That Mummy and Daddy were put on the *Aeroflot* plane as stretcher cases, but that they were more likely sedated than injured. That they will have to answer for crimes that she won't be able to understand until she is older – much older . . .

'Grandpa and grandma were involved in the political difficulties, they told me, and to try to contact them would only make things worse for them. I can't blame them for fobbing me off with half-truths and evasions . . . They had their own upheaval to cope with, and since it was for my sake, it doesn't behove me to hark back to what was said about what, and when. They changed their name to protect me. They set up a new home in Winchester, with everything new – nothing at all was brought from the old house. They cut themselves off from Highgate as if they'd never lived there. They sent us – Barbara and me – to school at Winchester . . .'

The wisp of cloud no bigger than the tip of a finger, which from the very beginning of Irina's story, he'd spotted in the otherwise blue sky of the Komarov–Cook relationship, was now blotting out the blue with the dark menace of Old-Firm involvement. It was easy now to supply the likely meaning of the words:

*NINE ONE ALSO REQUIRES YOU TO INFORM ZERO ZERO EIGHT OF TIMINGS TO ENABLE HIM TO TAKE PROTECTIVE ACTION. . .*

008 was Gerald Cook, and Komarov wanted him to be told exactly *when* he, Komarov, proposed to defect in Vienna, to give Gerald time to spirit Irina away beyond the reach of Soviet counter-measures . . .

' . . . But like the girl they kept away from spinning wheels and spindles, I stumbled eventually on the hidden and forbidden . . . I read a book which told the story of how my parents were denounced to our own people by an Englishman working for the KGB . . . This man was the author of the book, and his story was that my parents were on the point of defecting to Britain.'

'And were they?'

'I don't know. When I tackled the Cooks, their version was that it had long been my parents' intention to defect to the West. It had been a question of waiting for the right moment, and this had come in Vienna. My father's greatest concern had been that once they got wind of his defection, our

London embassy would do their best to get hold of me. With me as hostage, they could bring my father to heel.'

'But you weren't convinced?'

'I couldn't for the life of me see why they should attempt in Vienna what they could have done far, far more conveniently in London. My father was in constant touch with Gerald, who held some government research post. Gerald would have smoothed the way.'

'Do you believe your father wanted to defect?'

'I feel sure that he didn't. He loved Leningrad. So did mother. They were patriots. They were dedicated to our country.'

'Looking back, doesn't it strike you that your position in London – living apart from the rest of the embassy, attending an English school, fraternizing with an English family – was odd to say the least?'

'Of course it does. And I can't explain it. I don't know, but I suspect that my father was high up in our Intelligence service, that some involved operation was being prepared in which all of us – he, my mother, perhaps even I had some part to play . . . But that's what I suspect. It's no more than a feeling, and probably nonsense.'

'Did the Masons not put difficulties in the way of your Voronezh and Moscow trips?'

'Of course they did. It had never occurred to them, toasting my scholarship to Oxford, that a year in the Soviet Union formed part of the Russian course. The myth had been that *one* day, at twenty-one, say, I would be free to decide whether to stay in England or return home. When I told them of Voronezh I got a very firm no.'

'But you won?'

'My tutor won. He fought the battle for me, imagining my parents to be ultra-conservatives who didn't want their daughter contaminated. That put the Masons at a decided disadvantage. My own argument – to them – was that I couldn't make up my mind if I didn't know what the choice

105

was – I had, after all, spent more of my conscious life in England than I had in Russia. Well, they and those behind them let me go. Maybe they thought that even I would be taken in by the *Place of birth: Winchester* on my doctored passport. But the Cinderella-warning was that I was not to come to Leningrad. I wouldn't be equal to it emotionally, they thought.'

'Now they've relented even over that?'

She looked away. 'They think I'm in Venice. And so I was for a day or two – long enough to see the Bridge of Sighs. That's why I was late.'

'Is that being fair?'

'Fairness doesn't come into it!' Her face was hard. 'What obligation am *I* under to be fair? What are they to me? Friends, guardians, kind people – yes, they've been all that, but counterbalancing it all is that, in a sense, they've been my captors . . . And what am I to them? A means of salving their consciences for having got my parents into a mess? A pawn in some elaborate chess game I shall never be shown the true score-sheet of? There's only one particular I really know them to be right about – the unwisdom of my coming here. I'm not equal to it emotionally. I shouldn't have come. Without you, Nicholas, I think I would just have run . . . Straight back to Moscow, then Venice.'

'Run? Not given yourself up?'

'I certainly wouldn't have gone to the nearest *otdeleniye militsii*, said *I'm a Soviet citizen, comrades. My British passport's an official fake. What do you suggest?* I faced the impossibility of that as early as Voronezh . . .

'Oh, Nicholas, Nicholas, I'm in such a mess! Being me is like loving two men at the same time, both of them married, both of them with lives I don't and can't fit into . . . Not a recipe for happiness or success . . . It's too late now to branch out on my own. I've got in too much of a muddle.'

'Too late to fit into some sort of life in England? In Oxford?'

'The Isis isn't the Moyka. Blenheim's no Petrodvoryets. The Ashmolean to the Hermitage is a hut to a palace . . . My heart is here. The Little Mermaid suffered the agonies of walking on land of her own free will, out of love. The agonies I suffer walking Oxford instead of Leningrad are not of my own choosing. I suffer not in love but in hatred – hatred for those on both sides who dragged me out of my element.'

'Aren't you taking refuge in self-pity?'

'Pity – any kind of pity – is a bit of an emotional luxury, something you indulge in from a position of security and superiority – a position that's certainly not mine.'

'What happened last night to upset you, Irina?' he shot back. The hand on his arm tightened into a grip. The question hung in the air. He waited. The reddish-brown hippopotamus humps looked like lozenges dotted about a mirror. It seemed an age before she spoke, and her voice, when she did, was quiet and utterly toneless.

'Coming off the platform, you go down a few steps to the coach park. I happened to be on my own at that moment, wondering whether to go off with the others and have supper, after dumping our bags in the hall at the hostel, or chance finding you in your room. I heard Eleanor saying something in her clear Oxford tones, but it was a fraction of a second before, subconsciously, I computed the sounds into sense. And what I think she said was *Christ, Peter Grant with a bloody beard!* It took another fraction of a second to absorb the sense, and when I did, I saw she was looking at a car that was moving off, a common sort of car like the one we see when we're walking to breakfast.'

'What colour?'

'Red, scarlet, I'm not sure.'

'Who was Eleanor talking to?'

'Herself, I think.'

'Did *you* see who was in the car?'

She hesitated and swallowed. 'Yes, I did. That's the whole point. It was someone I've met several times at Valeriya

Borisovna's. Someone I feel I know. Lomashev, Pyotr Petrovich, a painter . . . '

'You're sure it was the same person? You saw him clearly?'

'He has a Solzhenitsyn beard, the sort you never see here.'

'Did you tell Eleanor she must be mistaken?'

'I couldn't have said anything to anyone at that moment. My heart was in my mouth. My head was in turmoil. *Supposing she's right!* kept hammering in my head. *Supposing she's right!* I managed to tell Carvel I was going to walk. All I wanted was to be alone . . . '

They walked as they had walked the evening before, hand in hand and in silence. They were within sight of New Peterhof railway station when they found their way half-barred by men and women wearing red armbands.

'Citizen, citizeness, proceed properly,' growled a deep bass voice. 'One must proceed properly, is that understood?'

Irina released his hand. 'Of course. We apologize, comrades.'

'We apologize,' Ashweald echoed.

The People's Volunteer Militia patrol nodded its stern satisfaction and marched vigilantly on.

'I must say I expected worse of Soviet Authority than that!' he said to break the silence.

Irina rounded on him. 'Because like all westerners you see us through a filter sensitive only to cruelty and inhumanity! It's as bad as looking at Britain and seeing only Dartmoor Prison. There's kindness here too, you know, and humanity and understanding . . . '

'I didn't mean to be thoughtless,' he said. 'I'm sorry.'

'And I'm sorry too. I've no right to vent my unhappiness on you of all people . . . '

'Excuse me, comrade . . . ' A young man standing by a telephone box asked Ashweald for change, which he was able to provide. As they walked on, Irina said suddenly, 'I know you love Russian. Every word you speak betrays that. Do you also love Russia? Enough to want to stay?'

'I think I love Leningrad enough to want to stay.'

'Do you? I don't know if I do any more. And that's after ten years here. How would I see it after a period of corrective training, I wonder, which is what I'd have to do to purge my parents' offence – whatever it was – and my own anglicization. I've had twenty years of England, yet I don't even know if I want to go back there . . .'

'And supposing you did stay, what sort of job would you like to have?'

She smiled. 'I know what I'd like to do – but they'd never let me – and that's read the Radio Moscow news in English, and in a proper tone of voice, not like a self-important teacher talking down to a remedial group of half-wits . . .'

'Would you enjoy what you had to read?'

'I expect not. But if I read it properly, people might listen and judge it for what it was, rather than switch off at the first few unctuous syllables . . .'

# 8.

The Leningrad train arrived crammed full, and but for irresistible pressure from behind they would never have got in. Inside they were subjected to pressures worthy of oceanic depths. To turn, reach for a handkerchief, feel for one's ticket or wallet was out of the question. It was only just possible to breathe, and where the effort of breathing left scope for it, there was nothing to do except think – about Irina and her story and Peter Grant and his.

When, after what seemed a very long time, the pressure relented, movement was restored and they stepped out onto the platform of the Baltic Station, Irina suggested that they should walk. 'I can be honest now and admit to knowing the way,' she said. 'And I know a good one that keeps beside water almost all the time . . . '

The sky was dim yellow, the street deeply shadowed, the breeze stirring the plentiful litter only mildly warm to the face.

'Tell me about Lomashev,' he said.

'He was at Valya's the first time – that evening you asked me to come on the Neva. He's been there every time since. Kolya – Valya's husband – is curator of the Repin Museum. They actually live in what was once Repin's house, or rather, they live in a restoration of what was once Repin's house. I thought I'd gone to the wrong place – it looked so grand, a rambling old-style *dacha* of the very wealthy. Valya led me in to meet her husband and one or two friends. It was like stepping into a scene from *The Seagull* . . . Except that there were about three times as many people sitting around and talking, and the subject was art, not literature.

'Lomashev's no Trigorin, though he has his admirers in tow. Most of the time he just sits, nodding assent but saying little. His Russian's odd. Not specially English, but then if you don't expect it to be you don't notice. I remember a *plyt'* for *plavat'* when he said he couldn't swim, but that's not a specially English mistake.'

'How did swimming come up?'

'He has the use of a boat. Valya said he ought to learn . . . She told me, after that first time, that he was a returned émigré who had to re-learn Russian late in life. I very nearly said that so was I a returned émigrée, but of course I didn't . . . I've got into the habit of vetting most things before I say them . . . Except with you. I like to think it's a prudent habit. But sometimes, when morale's low, I get a nasty feeling that deception comes naturally to me, that it's in my blood, a horrible legacy from my parents . . .

'I told you how when I got to Pulkovo I wanted to turn and run . . . It was because, coming home, I felt I had no defence, no disguise to cover me – no gym slip and boater, no college scarf, shapeless woolly and jeans. I felt that all that was most secret about me had been laid open with a knife. Then suddenly there you were, mistaking a Russian for me, and looking at me in astonishment when I said who I was . . . You made me laugh, you broke the spell of self-obsession. I thought you at once the nicest man I had ever met . . . With you here, I thought I might be able to manage . . . I couldn't have got this far without you . . .

'And now, I've told you what I have because things are bad, bad as they can be – I just can't keep bottled up in myself the implications for me in the fact that someone I know and have talked to is Peter Grant, *the* Peter Grant! And if I could, it wouldn't be fair to inflict on you moods of which you could have no understanding . . . '

'Can you, Irina, be absolutely sure that Lomashev in his

111

car was the man Eleanor thought was Grant?'

'There was the beard . . . And there was the look on his face – furtive, frightened – as if he'd spotted someone, and didn't want that someone to spot him.'

'Eleanor?'

'I don't know.'

'Could he have heard what she said?'

'Almost certainly not. It wasn't said very loud, and porters and people were passing between us and the car. The car was as far away as the other side of the road from here.'

'His window – was it up or down?'

'Down. He had his elbow sticking out – I remember the check shirt.'

'Where was Carvel?'

'I've no idea.'

'It wasn't to him that Eleanor spoke?'

'I don't think she was speaking to anybody.'

'Did she or anyone else mention Grant afterwards?'

'No.'

'Does Eleanor know of your visits to Repino?'

'She may know from Tatiana that I've been there, but not where. I've never mentioned the house or the people.'

'But Carvel must know the address, from that first time when you said you might stay the night.'

'He doesn't. You told me to tell him, Nicholas, but I didn't.'

'Why not?'

'I didn't find him in time.'

'Are you satisfied that Lomashev and Grant are the same?'

'Instinctively, I think I am. To be positive I'd have to take Eleanor along, and I can't do that.'

'If Eleanor's the journalist we think she might be, she'll be after a scoop . . . Anyone who can recognize Grant after all these years, and in spite of a beard, must have studied the Grant photographs long and hard. She'll have done a lot of delving, and she may – just may – have got some lead concerning you . . . '

'Yes, I can see that.'

'Will you go to Repino any more?'

'I'll have to ring Valya and make some excuse.'

'How much does it still matter whether this man is Grant?'

'It mattered very much when I realized I'd been walking and talking with my parents' killer . . . The only thing in the world that did matter. I was all for sweeping to my revenge. Like Hamlet. And it wasn't for their sake. They knew what they had let themselves in for . . . No, it wasn't for them, it was for me. I wanted revenge for my own satisfaction. Having been pitched into someone else's equation willy-nilly I wanted at last to play some part myself . . . '

'Do you still?'

'Yes, I do. In principle I do. Which I admit because, inside, I accept the stark impossibility of achieving any sort of revenge . . . I can't identify him with certainty – not without endangering myself. And even if I could, I wouldn't have the remotest idea how to go about killing him. You see – I *have* thought it out.'

'Yes.'

'Oh, you talk of self-pity, but you can't imagine what it is to be me! I'm not the dead child held aloft by the Hero-Mother of the monuments for all humanity to mourn. I'm the child victim who never got held aloft but went on living, at least outwardly . . . But inwardly I'm dying. Victim of a war I.knew nothing of. Like an irradiated baby of Hiroshima or Nagasaki.

'For twenty years I've longed, I've languished, I've yearned to walk this silly route we're walking now. Father discovered it. He'd taken me to Petrodvoryets. The train was a crush that day too. Probably always is. Need to stretch our legs, he said when we came out of the station. When we got to the Fontanka, he said let's see if we can keep beside the water all the way home. And now I am walking here once more, the agony seems worse, not better. I don't belong here. I can't belong. I look all right still, but something terrible's going wrong inside . . . Why, why should *he* live on happily, painting the home he has destroyed for me!'

Ashweald thought of Gretchen in *Faust* . . . The same corruption and destruction of innocence and sanity. Every time he taught it, the more immediate and overwhelming it seemed. He'd never teach it again. Not now. But could a destroyed human not be restored – like Petrodvoryets? No. Assuredly not by Man. Even so, Man must try . . . 'I remember Grant's book,' he said. 'I read it when it appeared. I wanted to know what crime could deserve fifty-six years' imprisonment. What especially struck me was the second half, which tells about prison life. The man who wrote that was aware, selfless, concerned. Not the kind to commit cold-blooded murder by proxy . . . '

'You don't have to be any-sort-of-blooded to commit murder by proxy – you just press the button, like the man in the bomber. Afterwards, you're left with nothing to forget – except pressing the button.'

'Except that I couldn't imagine him ever pressing the button.'

'So prison softened the swine!' Irina retorted. 'Is that what you're telling me?'

'Grant's treatment was savage – not calculated to soften.'

'And so I should hope!'

'My point is that the espionage part rings false, the prison part doesn't. That book is half ghost-writer, half Grant. To go nurturing thoughts of bloody revenge on the strength of a few pages of ghost-writer's invention is bloody silly. Bloody silly!'

She stopped abruptly, back to the embankment railings, drew him close, looked up beseechingly. 'Don't be angry, Nicholas. You're the last person I want to repel. Your friendship, your help, your sanity mean everything, every-thing . . . ' She pressed her face to his chest as if to shut out the world.

114

'Can't you see the sense of what I'm saying?'

Looking up again, wide-eyed, she drew his head down and kissed him repeatedly, inexpertly, in the manner of a child showing affection to a toy or pet, pecking rather than kissing, icy-lipped, back arched awkwardly over the railing. Beyond her hanging hair, the water too was black.

'Careful,' he said, 'or we'll end up in the Fontanka.'

'It's not the Fontanka. It's the Griboyedov Canal. And I don't care.'

Still no mail from England. Another week to wait for that, Carvel said, although heaven alone knew why, with England only four hours away. But on the *dezhurnaya*'s counter, amongst the many envelopes which no one claimed, those who might have done having long departed, Ashweald found a hand-delivered picture postcard addressed to himself, an atmospheric version of the Bronze Horseman in mist and snow against a copper sky. The message read:

> *Sorry can't manage this evening (Mon.) after all. Will be in touch soon. Glad you're enjoying the course and Lenin's city so much. Yrs BG.*

By which Peter meant Tuesday – tomorrow – evening. The short notice was surprising. Could it be that Peter too was not entirely unscathed by the encounter at the station? Could it be that he had been there to see for himself who was in the group? So much, in that case, for the notion of a neat KGB list showing what Britishers were attending what, where and for how long, with photographs affixed! In the Firm they had always credited their opposite numbers with super-efficiency. It had never crossed their minds that they might be being over-generous.

He lay on his bed, too oppressed by the revelations of the day even to open a can of Lager. Peter Grant and his works he had thought neatly pigeon-holed, leaving him free, when not with Irina, to keep an eye on Carvel and Eleanor. Free also to potter around from time to time in that darker corner of the mind where were stored the possibilities presenting themselves to a man possessed of a hundred and fifty thousand pounds sterling and the love of a young attractive girl . . . *As good as possessed*, was nearer the mark. Said young attractive girl might yet be carted off to a *gulag*. He himself might be seized following a nod and a wink from Peter. The bank holding the hundred and fifty thousand deposit might turn out to be a front for the Firm . . . But now Peter dominated the scene like a sky full of thunder clouds. The imminent flash-flood threatened to engulf them all.

He switched to Eleanor's microphone. Not a sound. The telephone microphone produced only the distant voice of the *dezhurnaya* rendered unintelligible by the echo and overlaid by the click of heels on the floor.

He poured himself a good four fingers of vodka, but seized with sudden repugnance, left the glass standing. Taking his stick, he let himself out into the corridor, descended the stairs two at a time, and unchallenged by the *dezhurnaya* went out into the night. It was even cooler now, and he stepped out briskly, heedless of direction.

He awoke to his surroundings in the great open expanse of Palace Square. There was the Alexander Column commemorating the victory over Napoleon, the point from which Irina's tutor had told her to find her way. Ahead gleamed the baroque cliffs of the Winter Palace and the Hermitage. He passed to the left of the Winter Palace through the little park with the fountain – not splashing at this late hour – came out onto Palace Embankment, and crossed to walk beside the river. Where, where else had municipal utility and municipal beauty ever been so tempered to the might and majesty of waters to produce such perfection? And so firmly rooted in the everyday were the grandeur and sublimity of this perfection, that the everyday partook of it willy-nilly and was transmuted. He began to understand Irina, and perhaps Peter, too. This was a master-piece amongst cities. A supreme fusion of Slavonic East and Latin West. Here was the place for East and West to meet for the good of the world!

Just beyond Kirov Bridge he crossed, as he had done with Irina, to the Summer Garden side of the road. Viewed at night from the pavement, the finest railings in the world were at their least impressive. He fell to counting the pillars supporting the railings, and got to thirty-five or thirty-six before some granite steps he'd not noticed by day led up to yet another little humpbacked bridge. Crossing the Fontanka he turned right and followed the embankment. Ahead he saw a bunched group of figures which he took to be another Volunteer Militia patrol until, drawing closer, he saw them locked in violent struggle. Supposing them to be drunks, he moved out into the road to give them a wide berth, but as he drew level he heard an unmistakable voice growling 'Leave him be, you buggers . . . ' And there was Ernie pulling one man off the back of another who was grappling with two other men, and before he knew it, Ashweald was moving in against the two attacking the one. Surprised, his opponent backed to the parapet where Ashweald, on sudden reckless impulse, grasped his ankles and toppled him into the Fontanka with a great splash. The man to whose aid he had sprung then catapulted his remaining attacker the same way. Ernie meanwhile, holding his man above his head like a bolster, walked unhurriedly to the parapet and dropped him over.

'*Spasibo, spasibo,*' the rescued man said, instantly betraying himself as an American.

Ashweald said in English that he was glad to be of service.

'Gee, but you sound British!'

'And so, I hope, do I,' Ernie threw in.

The American shook hands solemnly. 'Bill, Bill Steiner, Major, US Marines. Glad to know you, gentlemen. But what you say we hijack these hoodlums' jalopy, get ourselves clear

117

and save us a cab-fare?'

Ashweald slipped behind the wheel and started the engine. Ernie climbed into the back. 'Here's your walking stick. I went back for it. Just in time to poke one back down who was climbing up. They're treading water well. No cause for anxiety.'

Ashweald steered to Steiner's direction and soon arrived where he wanted to be. 'Can't thank you guys enough,' he said through the open door. Saved me from a put-up piece of provocation and got me back in time to establish an alibi . . . Just ask for me here when the smoke clears a bit, and collect yourselves a case of Bourbon. S'long . . . '

'Ee, but that toned me up a treat,' Ernie said when they had dumped the car. 'It was good you happened along. Yon heavies had it in for the Yank. Breed I can't abide, Yanks, but you can't just pass by and watch one getting thumped, now, can you?'

'And how does Yank-thumping square with your boundless admiration for things Soviet?'

'Just indignation of people, manifestation of . . . ' Ernie replied unabashed. 'Me, I sympathize with the theory, if not the practice.'

'Do we report this to Carvel?'

'That neo-fascist? Do we buggery! Hand us over to the beaks, Carvel will, and never bat an eyelid.'

'It was your fight, so it's for you to decide.'

'Can't see a People's Court taking a lenient view of heaving security men in the drink and driving away their vehicle without consent . . . '

'Mum's the word, then.'

'Mum's the word. Must say I admired your economy of effort, young Nick. And I had you written down as a non-games-playing weed . . . '

'Maybe your *neo-fascist* is just as wide of the mark.'

'Aye, you've a point there. Happen I'm over-free with the abuse . . . But establishment toadies I simply can't abide.

118

Get right up my nose, do establishment toadies. And he's one, from his inverted-calf shoes to his rolled-gold Parker . . . Funnels students into government service does Carvel, like a pimp!'

'And *you* disapprove because the Government's not Labour?'

'Don't give a duck's feather what colour the Government is. Government service means secret service for the Foreign Office, the War Office or some other tomfool office – work better not done. Yon Carvel's here to report back on every last one of us, I'll go a bundle on that . . . '

'What do you reckon Eleanor's angle is?' Ashweald asked. 'Does she report on us too?'

'Booze, baccy and if you'll pardon the French, bollocky males – that's Eleanor's angle. Oh, and she writes exclusives for a right-wing Sunday.'

'Doesn't recruit for government service?'

'Not that I know of . . . Old Eleanor must have done this course as many times as me. The first few times we used to rag her she was after *The Prize* . . . Every minute of our stop-overs in Moscow she'd run round like a blue-arsed fly looking through the windows of posh restaurants – that is, when she couldn't get in through the door.'

'What prize?'

'Aw, five, six, seven years ago – I can't remember – Eleanor's Sunday put up a prize – ten, twenty thousand, it may have been, I can't remember – for whoever spotted the spy Peter Grant and got a picture or an interview or something . . . '

'Does it still stand, this prize?'

'Ask Eleanor. Don't read her rag myself. Don't have much use for newspapers, me, except to stuff wet shoes with. I read the *Herald* once.'

Well before the hostel they split up, so as not to be seen entering together. Ernie wanted Ashweald to go in first, having had the greater strain of driving the getaway car, but

Ashweald said he felt like walking a bit longer.

'Any road, it were a grand tussle,' Ernie said. 'Second time you've come to my rescue.' And with a cheerful wave he turned away.

# 9.

Irina made no secret of her disappointment when Ashweald announced that he was invited somewhere for that evening. 'You're supposed not to know anyone here,' she protested. 'I think you're just paying me back for disappointing you over that evening on the Neva. I wish now I'd come.'

He'd far, far rather spend the evening with her, he said, but some people Eleanor had introduced him to had invited him back and didn't want Eleanor to know. He hated himself for lying, but perhaps one day Klavdiya and Kirill *would* invite him back without Eleanor . . .

'All right then, I'll meet you from the metro,' she laughed.

'That wouldn't be seemly. I might be delayed and keep you hanging about.'

'Can we at least have tea together?'

'Tea at the *Astoriya*, then a laze in the sun in the Summer Garden.'

'Perfect. Then tomorrow a whole evening together?'

'Tomorrow without fail.'

'So tonight I shall wash my hair, if the water's not too dirty, and perhaps return a bit of Tatiana's hospitality. Can I come and join you in your room for a *ploughman's* as you call it, for lunch?'

'I was going to scrap lunch and ring home.'

She pouted. 'I seem doomed to disappointment.'

'We'll be together at lessons this morning, and at Dostoyevsky's house this afternoon . . .'

His sense of foreboding was growing from the occasional,

easily dismissed twinge into an acute and persistent ache. Sun, lessons, excursions, jollity no longer entirely soothed it away. Rocks, rapids, whirlpools lurked ahead, still invisible, but no longer comfortably remote. He had no means of assessing the rate of drift, but felt that it was accelerating . . .

'Nicholas, you're not eating your breakfast . . . '

He was thinking suddenly of love – of the great march from griffon bridges, from Summer Gardens, through births, children's illnesses, death of pets, exams, driving tests, unsuccessful interviews, unsuitable attachments . . . On for ten, twenty years in his case, for forty or fifty in Irina's . . . His thoughts suddenly of these things, he was looking past her at the house where she had lived.

In the lunch break he extracted Eleanor's key together with his own, let himself into her room and stood considering the cases of drink, packs of cigarettes, scattered books. The hardest room to search in a hurry is the room in complete disorder. Typed sheets scattered around the small portable typewriter appeared to be a write-up of scattered sheets of pencilled notes – chatty, disconnected stuff, a travelogue. From beneath this stratum he extracted a cardboard folder. In it were coloured reprints torn from *Ogonyok* and similar publications, some of them quite old and tatty. Examples of modern Soviet art – Kondrashin, Utkin, Fyodorov, and, yes, Lomashev . . . Perhaps a dozen Lomashevs, interleaved with the rest. All dated. The earliest '78, the latest '82 . . . Courtyards, trees, parts of buildings viewed through trees, shadow patterns cast by foliage inside rooms, on walls, bookcases . . . Shadow patterns usually in motion, shivering, blurred, very precisely blurred, an impression of definite shape and mass in rapid movement. An obsession with foliage . . . As if the artist saw leaves as a living link between worlds, between earth and sky, as a near relative of the squirrel *ratatoskr* of Old-Germanic cosmology . . . A quality easily missed in the dead colours of the reprints by anyone who had not seen the living canvas of the Stroganov courtyard. But what was this? But he knew, knew at a glance, recognizing in a flash how clever, how methodical Eleanor had been. A drab, ugly yard in watercolours. Dead, flat, matt, dull. No life, except in the top right corner, a leafy branch, lime, projected in silhouette by a shaft of wan sunlight . . . He was no connoisseur, no expert, but there, unmistakably, even in crude water-colour, was the genesis of Peter's foliage technique. That grubby little rectangle of cartridge paper was an original! Part of the collection abandoned in prison. Signed *PLG*.

God, he could understand it now, that involuntary view halloo at the station! A sight of the quarry after years of hunting! Flicking through again, he found three more reprints – all of the Stroganov courtyard, but so insipid as to be barely recognizable.

Before opening the door into the corridor he hesitated, fearful of finding himself face to face with Eleanor or Helen Blore. Be bold! He swung open the door, stepped out, stooped to lock it and caught the eye of Carvel, similarly engaged at their door further down the corridor.

'Thought you'd gone off leaving the key behind,' Carvel said.

'I was fetching something for Irina.'

'Ah.'

From that sound he was unable to tell whether Carvel had noticed it was not Irina's door that he had emerged from. 'Join me in a Lager,' he suggested. 'There's time.'

'No, I've got to dash. Save it for me!'

Ashweald hoped that he would be in too much of a hurry to notice that Irina and Tatiana's key was still in its compartment of the drawer. He no longer felt easy in Carvel's company, no longer trusted the genial-Bard exterior and manner. *Yon Carvel's here to report back on every last one of us* . . . Why, knowing about bugging, did he allow others to be indiscreet for the benefit of hidden listeners, while himself committing exploitable indiscretions? If facts about the course leader were gold, the facts supplied by his many visitors would be gold galore . . . Was that how he wanted the Russians to look at it? If Carvel was still Firm, what better camouflage than a display of naivity and innocence? But if Carvel was still Firm, why hadn't Archie said so? Setting Firm against Firm was like putting mirror to face mirror . . .

Hell, the telephone! The telephone! He slipped on the headphones, set the cassette recorder running and switched to the microphone in the entrance hall. Echoing footsteps. Women's voices. A shout 'Yelena Andreyevna!' Then Carvel's precise academic Russian. 'Very good, Konstantin Arsenievich. I apologize, as I say, for such late notice, but I have been before. Twice . . . Yes, this afternoon. Professor Panteleimonov can't manage any other time . . . No . . . Very much obliged, Konstantin Arsenievich.' The receiver crashed down. Sound of Carvel walking away. He had not expected the other end of the conversation to be audible, but was still disappointed to find that it wasn't. Konstantin Arsenievich he guessed to be Chichibayev. Carvel was excusing himself the afternoon class and expedition . . .

He poured another Lager, spread processed cheese on a thick slice of black bread, took a deep bite. His eye lighted on the glass of vodka from the night before. A temptation the cleaners had apparently resisted. The leg of the wardrobe slightly to the right of its well-established depression in the carpeting testified to their ministrations. But no, they hadn't been! The waste-paper basket was still full of empty cans. Today was their exit-day. He eased the wardrobe away from the wall and soon located a radio microphone of a type similar to his own. He turned on the wall radio, selected a channel with speech and let himself into Carvel's room. His cassette recorder was switched off, no keys were depressed, but the little wheels were revolving behind their window. He returned to his own room, switched off the radio, then took another look at Carvel's cassette recorder. The wheels were now stationary. Carvel's equipment was therefore superior to his own to the extent of incorporating a voice-operated relay. Anything said in Ashweald's room would be automatically recorded in Carvel's. In the evening Carvel would run through the tape, then re-set it for next day. The recording would be on a track obtainable only by secret manipulation of the conventional knobs, a feature shared by Ashweald's own machine.

He glanced at his watch and moved fast. He deposited his key and Eleanor's in the drawer in the entrance hall, and half-way to the door stopped dead, remarked aloud in Russian that he'd forgotten his stick, and retrieved his key taking Irina's also.

He had never before been in her room, and now, intruding on her privacy in a way that he had never intended and felt uncomfortably guilty about, he determined to see and notice as little as possible. But amongst that little was a sketch of himself, the one Lady Tatiana had made and not shown him. Mounted on card it was propped against the lamp on the bedside table. He looked for some time, trying to decide what she had singled out as salient, before he saw. Sadness. Regret. Resignation. Or was it calm? Sitting by the picture was a teddy bear, face a little worn by owner affection. Its peasant blouse was buttoned at the neck, embroidered with stylized blossoms at the breast and gathered in by a belt at the waist. The breeches were of authentic cut, the boots of fine soft leather. Between the bear's expression and his own there was a distinct similarity.

He found the microphone, attached to the wardrobe exactly as in his own room. He wrapped it in a handkerchief and pocketed it. He thought of various noisy places where he might re-attach it, but instead threw it into the Griboyedov Canal. From there, regardless of the midday heat, he went quickly to the Stroganov courtyard, where, with Peter's piece of yellow chalk, he marked certain railings.

He arrived over ten minutes late for Oral Practice with

125

Anna Dmitrievna. He apologized courteously, was, as he had anticipated, being Anna Dmitrievna's favourite, charmingly forgiven and motioned to the one vacant seat.

'Tortoises thriving?' Irina whispered, while Anna Dmitrievna wrote on the board.

The young student who took them round the Dostoyevsky Museum was not the usual sort of guide. He reeled off the facts he had been schooled to reel off, but in a way that encouraged comment and question. He knew the man, knew the things assembled in the museum, but above all he knew and understood the work of the man, good-humouredly conveying his conviction that the work was what mattered most. The flat, the study, the drawing-room, the things in them, were but empty shells on the shore; where the *man* now resided was in those masterpieces launched upon the living sea that pounded against that shore . . .

He was tall, lean and handsome. He and Irina would have made a good pair. He evidently thought so too, and conveyed as much in his manner of answering her questions, while she, gently but unmistakably, contrived to fend him off.

Amongst the English translations displayed, Ashweald was surprised and delighted to find copies of his own, made in the first years of his marriage – *Poor Folk*, *The Double* . . . So all these years part of him had been here, in Dostoyevsky's city, on this shelf . . .

'Why so solemn?' Irina asked in a whisper.

He handed her *The Double*, pointing to the date of acquisition. 'See – I was here the year you left, and have been ever since . . .'

She turned the pages. 'I like your translation. Especially this:

*It was a dreadful night, a real November night, dank, misty, rainy and snowy, a night pregnant with colds, agues, quinsies, gumboils and fevers of every conceivable shape and size . . .*

*The wind howled through the streets, lashing the black waters of the Fontanka high above the mooring rings, and vigorously rattling the feeble lanterns along the embankment . . .*

Even I forget there's another side to Peter the Great's creation . . . '

They had tea at the *Astoriya*, at a round table in the pokey cafeteria where American voices vied with Russian, and an electric samovar encouraged some to top up their glasses of tea and sit indefinitely, aggravating the crush.

In the Summer Garden they watched a descendant of Akhmatova's swan admiring his counterpart's beauty on the surface of the Carp Pond, and they walked beneath the shade of the limes. Already, here and there, a leaf had fallen or was falling. 'But we shan't be here,' Irina said, 'to see them all change colour and fall, or to see the statues boxed in, or the first carpet of snow . . . '

At the signal for closing time they headed slowly and reluctantly towards the southern gate and Ashweald's tram-stop. The swan was still admiring the beauty of his counterpart. What would happen when the Carp Pond was covered in ice?

He wanted so much to make her laugh, wanted to chase away melancholy as he had done before. But for once he could not overcome his own depression at the thought that in two hours' time he'd deliver himself up to Peter Grant, surrender the initiative, accept the type of gambit he had refused when Kirill offered it. He could tell no one where he was going. He didn't know. He could tell no one who he was going to see. In less than ten minutes from now, he would shake hands with Irina, board a tram – a No. 2, 3, 12 or 34 – and, for all he knew, vanish from Leningrad as completely as Peter had vanished from Parkhurst. The truth would never be known, however much money papers might offer, because there was no truth, and never had been, but only the semblance. He was going to see Peter, but he did not know why. The thought that it might be purely for the sake of a picture he brushed away whenever it came, like a troublesome fly. It was as persistent as a fly. Did that make it the real reason?

'Here's a No. 3,' he said, glad to break the silence. 'That'll do.'

'Let me come.'

'You're to go home and wash your hair.'

She pouted. 'Kiss me goodbye.'

'No. You'll get us arrested for immorality, unculturedness or something.'

'It'd be worth it,' she called after him.

He waved and watched her out of sight, craning his neck awkwardly, before depositing his three kopeks and tearing off a ticket.

In no time the tram was crossing Kirov Bridge, and the view he and Irina had admired, returning from the cemetery, he now looked at alone. He would tell her, if he ever saw her again, how subdued, northern and no longer Italian it looked, seen in the evening light . . . But she would say simply, *I know*.

He alighted at Kamenno-Ostrovsky Bridge, and to kill the time he had in hand, set off to walk the roundabout route he had planned from the map. Busy with his thoughts, he paid little attention to his surroundings, but one chestnut-lined avenue he noted in particular. An avenue of detached houses in spacious grounds, mini-châteaux that would have blended in well with those of the Hietzing District of Vienna or the Grunewald suburb of Berlin. Large dogs stood on terraces sniffing the air, large cars stood shining on the gravel. Tall walls, tall metal gates were the rule.

He checked to see if anyone was following but nobody was. No path could be straighter, more open, more easily surveyed over its total length than that which he followed into Victory Park in the direction of the Kirov Stadium. Anyone tailing here would stand out like a pillar box on an empty beach. That plant with the wild-rose-like flower lining the path was something he'd never seen in England.

The view from the high ramparts of the stadium was astonishing, an immense panorama of sea and city, sea and tree-lined coast, sea and modern buildings, sea and older, more beautiful buildings, expanses of beach and rock, and, over all, an immense sky. Any man led to this place and told to choose between it and all the kingdoms of the world, would be tempted indeed. London, New York, might testify to the same human power, but not – assuredly not – to the same human readiness to live in balance with nature, allowing nature to be the grander, the more powerful . . .

Thirty minutes to go. He was alone on his vantage point. The few people passing below were going about their own affairs. Twenty minutes later he was traversing the little Finland of greenery and water that is Yelagin Island. Half-way across the final footbridge, he paused to watch the rowers. Here there were more people, but all coming in the opposite direction. Still no one following.

He spotted the car park, the temple, the red *Zhiguli* simultaneously, almost on the dot of nine. Peter opened the rear door. 'Hop in, and get down on the floor. It's not far.' It was an unpleasant sensation being swung and bounced as if blindfolded. It was a relief when the car stopped and Peter said 'OK. We're here.'

They were parked overlooking a large, single-storied *dacha* with a balcony which appeared to run the whole way round. On three sides the *dacha* was bordered at a distance by mature firs and birches. On the fourth, it was open to the sea. Yellow, sun-scorched grass ran down to a stony beach, where a motor boat lay on a trolley.

'Yes,' Peter said, 'we're on the Gulf, and you can see roughly where. But it doesn't matter. It's not my *dacha*. I just have the use of a couple of rooms. Come into my parlour . . .' He unlocked the door at the head of the steps and led the way through the house to a large room facing the sea. The walls were taken up with books, the floor with easels and small tables bearing tubes of paint and slabs of glass on which paints had been mixed. Canvases were everywhere, their faces turned to whatever they happened to be propped against.

'Let's sit on the balcony. What do you fancy – white wine or red?'

'White, please.'

'White it shall be. Won't offer you the local beer – one part golden syrup, two parts sugar-water, with a dash of flat Guinness and a tot of anti-freeze. Confers headaches, blurs vision, promotes vomiting, does nothing for thirst . . . Cast an eye over the picture if you like . . . '

The detail was about two thirds complete. This was Peter at the height of his powers. The sun, the sun in the leaves – not only of the birch – was the source of the magic of the Stroganov courtyard, and he had immortalized a moment of that magic. Merely to glance at the picture was to live, breathe, feel the reality: the heat reflected by the palace, blocked by leaves, or let through by their trembling; the rippling patterns of their shadows; the radiant warmth of dully polished railings; the shivery cool of marble.

The room looked like someone else's study made over for Peter's use. The books bore mathematical and scientific titles conveying nothing to the layman. Opening one, he turned the fly-leaf to the light of the window, and in utter disbelief read and re-read the scrawl as *Martov*. The other books he examined were inscribed with the same name. So this was the *dacha* Kirill mentioned as the place where Ashweald might read his manuscript. How, in so many years, could Eleanor have failed to stumble on this arm of the maze and find her way to Peter? Kirill's *There is much we do not tell Eleanora Robertovna* acquired new significance.

A shelf of notebooks caught his eye at the same moment as the distant sound of returning footsteps caught his ear. They were of the hard-cover, many-paged variety favoured by students. He just had time to read the label of one, replace it and seat himself on a cane chair on the balcony before Peter came in. The name of the student was Klavdiya Pavlovna Komarova! A common surname, a common patronymic, a common Christian name . . . It could be dismissed as coincidence . . . Or it could be accepted as the fact it most probably was – that Klavdiya, Klavdiya Pavlovna, was the sister of Irina's father and so Irina's aunt . . .

# 10.

Peter set down a tray of glasses, bottles labelled *Tsinandali* in Georgian and Cyrillic script, and a large plate of black-bread cubes supporting chunks of salami and pickled cucumber. Decorating the centre of the tray was an oval scene in the manner of Breughel – the Neva at Kirov Bridge, frozen over, with people disporting themselves in various ways.

'I'd like to spear the *zakuski* to the bread with toothpicks *à la office party*, but toothpicks are in short supply . . . Still like the picture?'

'It's a masterpiece.'

'Well, if it finishes anything like it's started, I shall be moderately pleased, which is something I'm not very often . . . Bottle at your elbow. Dig in.' He ate hungrily, pausing only to drain and refill his glass. After a third refill he sat back, wiped his mouth on the sleeve of his red-and-white check shirt. 'Bloody long time since I spoke any English. Doesn't come to mind so readily as it should. Bit like my Russian. Local Dennis the Dachshund, that's me. Bit of a laugh, that, when one reason for coming – a big one if I'm honest – was wanting to be better at Russian than you . . .'

Not knowing how seriously to take him Ashweald said nothing. Peter of the beard seemed as prone to speechify as Warburton of the moustaches.

'I remember, Nick, an essay you wrote in the Sixth on Schiller's *Tell* . . . One point was that the grand, fateful, irrevocable act may spring – often by accident – from some homely, personal, selfish, comparatively trivial motive. Tell assassinates Gessler, you said, not to strike a blow for all his fellow Swiss or give the signal for a national uprising, but because Gessler endangers the life of his son. Much the same goes for quitting the Firm for the sake of Mother Russia. Some come to it through buggery, some through class disaffection, some through surfeit of naivity . . . But I, product of a grammar school fostering none of those peculiarly British accomplishments, achieved it via the ignoble wish to be one up on you . . .

'I remember – almost to the day and hour – your helping me out over a piece of recorded Russian I couldn't make sense of after trying for a whole day. You took the headphones, jotted it down as you listened. It might have been Dialogue 1 of a BBC course, not broadest Moscow dialect competing with echo and distracting noise. And it wasn't just that you understood, but that you clearly had sympathy, fellow feeling with them . . . I could see – you went along with them in emotion as well as in sense . . . I wanted to do that too. So I worked at Russian, harder than ever at Cambridge, but without ever getting that extra dimension you seemed to possess as of right, you and your acolyte Archie . . .

'I remember you'd stay in the office for days on end, sometimes sleeping there, to get on top of something even you found tricky. All I could do to help was go out and buy your sandwiches – chicken and chutney, banana – while Sue saw to the coffee . . . With that little electric mill that waltzed around the table . . .

'Solving problems, playing tungsten tip at the sharp end of Intelligence, was the one thing, you said, that stopped you seeing the fatuity of the industry as a whole. The main thing, you said, was to solve the problem for its own sake and the greater glory of your own experience, and never, never worry what, if anything, became of the product your problem-solving produced, because the short answer was: nothing. That way, you said, lay job dissatisfaction. But that was the way *I* had to go, having nothing to take satisfaction in, nothing to glow inwardly over . . . '

'You had your cartoons of the office blimps . . . I remember one you did of the DDI and party touring the *Lucky Dip* set-up, looking like governors going round a school – irrelevance personified. You were an artist, Peter, why the hell wish to be a linguist?'

'I wasn't an artist then. Not in any way that satisfied me. I had nothing, so I had to create myself something to feel secure in – an after-life to enter into when my time with the Firm ran out, and to serve as a counter-irritant and make my time with the Firm more supportable. I took an interest in our work. I even seemed, after you left, and to those who knew no better, to be doing a good job. But that was only to be able to report as much and as accurately as I could . . .

'Raskolnikov thought that by stepping over the bounds and doing murder, he'd gain a great sense of liberation, but found that he didn't. I must say I liked what I felt after my stepping over. Always, against my new life of tension and danger, I had the assurance of a better life to come, of speaking better Russian, of using Russian to some real constructive end, and never again artificially and dishonestly. You saw even then the reality of that world apart of which Russian is the ultimate expression. If I'd done that, things might have been different. I'd not have spent so many years living only for the sound of the coffee trolley in the morning and the tea trolley in the afternoon . . . '

'And how is it, this after-life?'

'My Russian's no better. But I do know Russians and something of Russia . . . And I find solace in painting . . . ' Averting his head he wiped eyes and nose on his sleeve. 'Sorry, but emotion will out . . . The last fellow-countryman I spoke to was in Parkhurst, the day I left . . . Subject for an etching, the Prodigal reversed: *Weeping Defector greets long-lost Chum* . . . ' He wiped again, and took breath. 'Hammer and Sickle, you'll have noticed, don't exactly bring home the bacon in the shape of tissues, hankies or bogpaper . . . I wondered for the first few days why you see people queueing to buy *Pravda* and *Izvestiya* and the rest, but you hardly ever see anyone reading them. The answer, as I soon found, is that they're not bought to be read . . . ' The corkscrew, as he opened another bottle, did not seem particularly well adapted to drawing corks. 'Done the Hermitage yet?'

'Not yet.'

'Mind you do. Veritable Aladdin's cave of art, even though some of it is badly hung.'

For a while they ate and drank in silence. The balcony, like the interior of the *dacha*, was heavily scented by the timber of which it was made, and the timber, as with Alpine chalets, seemed not only to shelter but also to protect.

'At Gwithian once,' Peter said, his voice suddenly as distant as Cornwall itself, 'Humphrey led me to a dying gull. He was only a Cairn, Humphrey, but for anything living, dead or remotely edible, he had a Labrador's nose. The gull had been winged, probably by some idiot who mistook it for a pigeon. I put it out of its misery. I hate killing – even the moths and midges that get in the way of the car. It was a Brown-headed Gull. Then I saw it had a ring. Took ages to get it off – bloody illogical, but I couldn't bear to damage the dead gull. It was so delicate, so perfect. Also I was beginning to hate myself for not trying to tend it, for thinking selfishly of the effort needed to look after and feed an injured bird. Twelve hundred miles it had flown, according to the ring, from Finland . . . I must say I felt a bit like that gull the morning you came bearing down on me at the Stroganov Palace. Except that when my time comes there'll be no ring to tell how far I've flown.'

'There'll always be your book.'

'What book?'

'*Lone Battle, the Odyssey of a Secret Agent.*'

'*Lone Battle?*' The incredulity seemed genuine enough, but Ashweald would not have sworn to it. Peter sat wide-eyed, cheeks bloodless, like the hero of *The Double* confronted by his usurping counterpart. The alien theatricality of manner stirred feelings of mistrust. 'A book by me?'

'It's got your name on the cover.'

'But I've never written any bloody book! What the hell have *I* got to write a book about?'

'Gwithian boyhood? Dawning of economic and political awareness? Blossoming of same at Cambridge? Life with the Firm? Prison? Aren't they enough to write a book about? Someone has.'

'Not me.'

'In which case you rake in a packet in damages.'

'Say rather that I might, were I not so placed. Who published it?'

'MacTavish.'

Peter whistled. 'Whose is the copyright? Who gets the royalties?'

'I never thought to look.'

'Tells about the Firm, you say? Does it tell the truth?'

'It's more like the spy-fiction of the day – real-sounding, but real rubbish.'

'Fiction then?'

'Fiction interlarded with pointers. You recognize communism as the only hope for humanity. Communism, you decide, deserves to win. You therefore fight for it in the secret war which the forces of reaction wage ceaselessly against it. Arrest, trial, sentence, you knock off in a few lines. After which you describe your time in Parkhurst. That bit is vivid and moving. Whoever wrote that has hit your style off pretty well.'

'More likely some sod's got hold of my prison diary. Which I started in solitary to keep myself sane . . . When I came out of solitary I kept it going – to give balance and a bit of contrast . . . I wasn't sure really which was worse – solitary or the company of my fellows . . . I can't see by what right the prison people handed that diary over . . . There were a lot of paintings as well . . . . I can't see why anyone would want to write a book posing as me. It doesn't make sense.'

'Given the mystery of your disappearance and your silence since, it could have the purpose of adding a bit of detail to the general blackening achieved by the trial . . . Or it could have been a device to trick you into reacting and so betraying your whereabouts . . . '

He refilled his glass, swung it in vicious circles on the table, tossed it down like vodka. 'Still, I don't suppose it was exactly a best-seller.'

'It certainly raised old dust again for a while. *Where is he? How did he get there? What's wrong with our security?* The leader writers, the reviewers, the TV and radio commentators had a field day. *Bafflement arises from the continuing ideological pull of the Soviet Union* . . . high-sounding sentiments of that sort . . . '

'No bright bugger suggested the pull of the real McCoy – the insidious charm of the Russian language?'

'Spies to us have become like Jews to the Nazis – they're not to be allowed any normality, any resemblance to ordinary decent people. Spies have got to be disposed of, mercilessly.'

'A lot must have argued that Peter Grant deserved to be disposed of mercilessly.'

'Oh yes. *Fifty-six years for fifty-six agents sent to their deaths* . . . '

'They said that?'

'One paper did. One that should have known better.'

'But bloody hell! The whole Old-Firm cast of thousands world-wide would have been hard put to parade you a *dozen* agents all told!'

'We know that. But papers and their readers don't.'

Peter sighed, leant back in his chair, ran a hand through his hair and looked thoroughly miserable. 'When you survive one injustice it's not pleasant to get still others chucked after you, as if the first wasn't enough. And I really can't see who's served by it. *Lucky Dip* was my one big egg. I gave *Lucky Dip* away. All right. That was stealing. That was wrong. But after

137

that I was no golden goose. I wasn't in any position to be. I wasn't in the same class as you or Archie. I reckon the judge was tipped to give me the sentence he did. And the sole purpose of that was to impress upon the world that Britain must be in possession of some stupendously important secrets . . . It wasn't the Firm. They were as shaken as me. They knew as you knew and I knew that five to ten years was what my crime was worth . . . Incidentally, does the book say how I was caught out?'

'No. How were you?'

'I've no idea. That's why I ask.'

'The book has you phoning an embassy contact to make an emergency letter-box clearing at your flat, but doesn't say that that was what dished you.'

'I don't think I'm going to read this book. It might, as you suggest, tempt me into the open – to clap a writ on bloody MacTavish!'

'You say you've no idea what gave you away?'

'I mean I don't know for sure. I've got ideas. One is that the Firm may have taken backbearings off a leak from some Russian source. But apart from *Lucky Dip* I passed nothing spectacular. I was biding my time hoping for the sort of break that would let me clean up and get out.'

'To Russia, you mean?'

'Before I got too old.'

'When you say you passed nothing spectacular, do you mean you give the Komarov affair a run-of-the-mill sort of rating?'

'The what affair?'

'Komarov.'

'Never knew a Komarov.'

'Sure?'

'I'm not so far gone that I can't remember what I've written or who I've tangled with! Products were my pigeon, not cases. If – Komarov or whoever – had walked through my door I'd have had kittens on the spot.'

'You weren't, when arrested, organizing the reception of a defector?'

'No.'

'No Komarov featured in the charges against you?'

'No.'

'Our pal, the Director, didn't, on the morning of the 13th September '64, call you into his office and show you a pink signal from Vienna?'

Peter flared into anger. 'Christ, but you've got your facts off bloody pat for someone unconnected with the Firm who's turned up purely by chance!' These final words he pronounced with venom. 'So what's the game, Nick, what's the game? I couldn't tell you how many times I flushed the bog on the morning of the thirteenth either!'

'I expect not. But there's no game. I got the facts from reading a German translation in your Saltykov-Shchedrin Library last weekend.'

'Why did you do that?'

'To refresh my memory.'

'Why?'

'I had the idea that if we met again, it would probably come up . . . We never thought you'd written it, Sue and I . . . I hoped I might find out for sure . . . I think I have.'

Peter seemed mollified. No, he hadn't been sent for by D – he wasn't in that sort of league. He did have a jolly to Vienna, though. In the second week of September. Hot as hell. It was on his return that he'd been arrested.

'What sort of jolly?'

'To replace Tommy Dawson for a few days. Tommy was off sick. His job was to scan *Lucky Dip*, before despatch, for nasty shocks. Warburton actually asked for little me. Shows how we were scraping the barrel for Russianists.'

'Did you see much of him?'

'Not after the initial handshake and beery grin.'

'You'd better have a look at the book some time.'

'When the coast's clearer I may. Fan the old embers back

into flame. Though I can't see much point. Forgeries gather dust just as fast as originals. Water under the bridge and all that, now, you might say.'

'You still need to be careful.'

'What of?'

'Reward hunters, for a start. For years now there's been a newspaper reward on offer. Whoever locates you comes in for a hefty five-figure sum. There must still be quite a few hoping hard to cash in.'

'You, for example?'

'All I want of you, Peter, is a picture. As to the rest, I'm not sorry that you escaped. I'm not sorry that you're here and happy. I, I promise you, will do nothing, here or in England, to drag you back into the limelight . . . '

'All right. I must accept that and be grateful. I only wish I could feel a bit more convinced. What I miss, what I don't quite spot, is the homely, personal, selfish, comparatively trivial motive, to use your phrase . . . '

'I left not because *I* took against the Firm, but because Sue did. Sue was always quicker with the correct reaction than I was. I react now in the way I believe Sue would react.'

'You were lucky in Sue . . . You had a son?'

'A son and a daughter.'

'Russian scholars?'

'Geoffrey is. Margaret's a physicist.'

'Going to keep Geoffrey clear of the Firm?'

'Geoffrey'll keep himself clear. He's too fond of Russia.'

'Will you marry again?'

'I don't think so.'

He drank off his glass of wine, then slid down comfortably in his chair, legs straight out in front of him, hands in pockets. 'All right. Point taken. I'll be careful. *More* careful. It's certainly not my aim to get winkled out of this shell on some smart Alec's pin . . . That's why I ran a wary eye over your course last Sunday when they all came trooping off the Tallinn train. And just as well. Carvel. I spotted Carvel. After your time Carvel was. We shared an office for a bit.'

'You saw the chalk marks?'

'Chalk marks? Christ, no!' There was a falter of anxiety in his voice.

'One of our party – not Carvel – has a folder of Lomashev reproductions cut from magazines over a period of years. In amongst them is what looks like an original from Parkhurst – drab yard with a few leafy branches intruding top right.'

Peter gazed unseeingly out at the Gulf. 'He's shown you all this? Explained how quick he's been on the up-take, bla, bla, bla . . . How the bloody hell did he get hold of it?'

'She – not he – doesn't know I've seen the folder. The moment I stumbled on it I went and chalked the warning. This afternoon.'

'Stumbled? Well, good for you and your nasty underhand Old-Firm ways! Have their uses, don't they? By God they do! So Lomashev's got to be every bit as canny and careful as Grant . . . Which is not to say that he isn't, usually . . . '

'It means keeping clear of Lomashev's known haunts.'

'I can see that.'

'This being one?'

'This place is known to three people only . . . My guardians, as I call them – who rank as trusties – and you . . . But gosh, empty plate, empty bottles, empty glasses . . . Hold your water a mo while I go in search of some seconds . . .'

The sea stretched away, placid and silent. The last of the sun was fading from the sky, but its warmth still lingered. Across the water, the lights of Leningrad glittered. He thought of Irina drying her hair. Of Irina and Lady Tatiana talking evenly, indefatigably, in the manner of Russian women. Of the picture that *was* Russia. Of all that he was not going to tell Archie when he got back. And, inconsequentially, of his son in Vienna, and of his daughter coping with the tortoises, the dog and the cat.

The tray came back loaded with garlic sausage, a black

loaf, a giant tomato, a bottle of vodka and cut-glass *ryumki* for its consumption. Peter poured vodka, then began slicing sausage, loaf and tomato.

'The perceptive lady with the folder – who is she? I didn't ask. Not, I trust, Lady Oakhurst?'

'Name of Archer-Smythe, Eleanor Archer-Smythe.'

He winced and turned so pale that Ashweald sprang up reaching for a handkerchief, fearing he had cut himself. Peter motioned him back to his chair and sat down himself. 'I'll finish slicing in a minute . . . Have some vodka . . . ' He drank three in quick succession and poured a fourth which he left standing. 'Don't suppose you remember Veronica. Veronica Mackenzie . . . '

'Joined shortly before we left? You brought her to our farewell do. Tall, fair, willowy, madonna face . . . '

'Good memory, Nick . . . That's Veronica. This Eleanor of yours – she is Veronica's sister. I never met Eleanor. Eleanor never approved of Veronica's husband. She approved even less of our living in sin pending Veronica's divorce . . . History don, or something? Oxford?'

'And free-lance journalist.'

'You see! *There's a divinity that shapes our ends . . .* Is there not? If I'd not bumped into you, Eleanor would surely have bumped into me, and I'd have been scuppered.'

'What happens if people inquire for Lomashev at the Society of Artists, or in *Gostiny Dvor*?'

'They get given an address, but it doesn't lead straight to me. That side's long been taken care of. What beats me is how the bitch got her claws on what I imagined safely forgotten in some screw's locker.' He got up and resumed slicing.

'Wish you and Sue could have known Veronica better . . . After your party broke up, we went off for a curry – no need to tell you where . . . I was hoping you two would end up there and join us . . . '

*Where* was Shafi's, Old-Firm territory, where the music

was as exotic as the dishes, long, long before exotic music became commonplace in London. And Peter had taken Veronica there, perhaps for their first meal together, as Ashweald had taken Sue . . .

So long ago . . . They must have been working late in their separate offices, for the sun was low, shafting almost horizontally across the road at the far end of the terrace where their branch of the Firm lived, and the road was empty, except for Sue at the bus-stop reading *The Manchester Guardian*. Recognizing each other as Firm they said hello. 'You're lucky,' he said, for there was a newspaper strike, and only *The Manchester Guardian* was to be had, and then only by regular readers. 'Take it,' Sue said, 'I've finished,' which wasn't strictly true because, like him, she kept the paper to be a companion at supper. They climbed to the top deck of the bus and rode, now in sun, now in shade, through the calm evening streets, chatting. Sue, younger than Irina now. Beautiful in a different way. Trafalgar Square, where they alighted, as magical, as pulse-quickening as Palace Square here in Leningrad. 'Would you care to join me in a curry, or some western dish if you prefer . . . ' Shafi's with Sue. The wonder, the all-enhancing wonder of awakening love . . . Sue and Nicholas. Veronica, Peter.

' . . . And all too soon we became close,' Peter was saying. 'Not right. Not fair. Wrong of me, wrong, all things considered. But part of me, deep down, had an urge for companionship, an irresistible urge for warm, everyday normality. None of the old *spring on the cheeks, winter in the heart* for me . . . Not a bit. I felt fine. Just fine. Civil servant to the world. Major, KGB, to myself. Like a perpetual bellyful of champers, it was – the real stuff, not this local fizz! With that inside there was nothing I couldn't do! Climb the Eiger, walk on hot coals, marry Veronica and live happily ever after . . . Nothing!

'You must know more about feminine psychology than me . . . But what I've never ceased to wonder is how Veronica

143

managed to guide me the way I should go, as she never managed to guide her husband. I packed in smoking, eased off drink, ate healthily, kept sensible hours, bought a flat. A sort of Super-Sonya she was, to my Raskolnikov. But I never found Raskolnikov's courage or honesty . . . I never came clean . . . I don't think I ever felt the urge to . . . It never seemed a crime – keeping high on the champers of your choice . . . Just exhilarating . . .

'What I said about Russian wasn't to butter you up, or put you off the scent. When I stood on the brink it was that that I thought of . . . It was that that steeled me to jump . . . The bugger is that what you know all too well about jumping off cliffs doesn't come through all that loud and clear when you're standing there and the oppo's making its urbane approach. You don't see the cliff edge, don't see that one step forward there is every bit as irrevocable.

'Do I regret taking it, you ask . . . I regretted it in Moscow, where they billeted me first. Chekhov's sisters were lucky they never got there. Red Square, Kremlin, good galleries, a piddling little river, and that's it. I loathed the translating job they gave me. Hours I'd spend getting something just right, then some idiot editor with about as much English as I've got Russian would blue-pencil the lot into nonsense. I smoked, boozed, wished I was back in Parkhurst. The people whose *dacha* this is bucked me up, got me on my feet – God knows why. They're both KGB – the human face of the KGB, you might say . . . Anyway, they've helped me, saved me, made me – keeping an eye on me at the same time, I suppose, but not very noticeably . . . I'm not supposed to contact any foreigner, so they wouldn't be exactly joyed to see us at the moment . . . They keep an eye on me, I keep an eye on their *dacha*. No need to look so worried, Nick. It's not bugged. Really not. More vodka . . .

'Kirill's an Academician. Walks with kings here and abroad. He it was who sold me the idea of studying art in Leningrad . . . Better hidey-hole than Moscow, less frequented by the ungodly . . .

'And Leningrad's been the catalyst . . . Love at first glimpse it was, stepping out of the station at God knows what hour of the morning. I saw my first Leningrad skyline, took my first breaths of Leningrad air, and was hooked for the rest of my natural . . . I love this city, I believe in it, and to that extent I love and believe in Russia. I want to paint Leningrad as no one has ever painted Leningrad before. I ask no more of life than to be spared to do that – show the world what manner of city it is, persuade the world of its worth, the quality of its people. What matter if the beer's undrinkable, with such beauty to intoxicate the eye!' He stopped short, like an old man feeling a twinge of age and infirmity temporarily forgotten. 'But the other side, the inevitable shadow to the light, is remorse – bitter black agonizing remorse, the mood of a kind of solitary confinement of the soul . . .

'The morning they rejected my appeal, Veronica went back to our flat, put down food for the cat for several days, swallowed a bottle of sleeping tablets and a bottle of whisky. Twenty to thirty years it would have been, with remission, before we could have begun the life together we wanted. Too late for children. I tell you, if I'd been writing that book I'd have had a hell of a lot to say about that . . .

'It wasn't the journal, you know, that kept me sane in those years of solitary . . . What kept me sane was that I accepted those years as part of my punishment – for causing Veronica's death . . .'

Ashweald let the silence lengthen before changing tack and asking, 'Where was it you were arrested?'

'Heathrow.' The reply was just a shade over fast. 'My only luggage being a briefcase, I came straight from the plane into that sort of cattle run where people wait to see if you're who they want . . . I spotted one of the Firm's drivers, never thinking I might be the lucky man, but damn me if he didn't make signals to the contrary. Bloody good show! Me for promotion, I thought. The car was slap outside, where you're not supposed to park. Four-litre Jag, the latest. God, I think of it with nostalgia when I'm driving that spin-drier *Zhiguli*! Looking on was an admiring group of Bobbies, arms folded regulation manner. The Jag turned out to be a Special Branch job. Usual lofty preamble: We are police officers, bla-bla-bla. Just the one charge at that stage, that between certain dates, *for a purpose prejudicial to the interests of the state, I communicated to another person information which might have been directly or indirectly useful to an enemy* . . . Three more sets of dates got thrown in later, to form four distinct charges.'

'The guilty plea – was that your idea?'

'I saw no reason not to be frank – within limits. Apart from which, it's expected, apparently, by both sides – like walking when the umpire gives you out. The Firm were all in favour. *Guilty* will soften the judge, they said, get the whole thing over and done with quickly and tidily.'

'The Firm being who?'

'Warburton.'

'Why Warburton?'

'*Lucky Dip* was his garden, as they say. Who better to assess just how badly I'd ploughed it up? Bloody good father confessor – soulful brown eyes, nose resting on that moustache . . . Like a horse looking over a hedge.'

'How did he take your ploughing up?'

'Tight lipped. No animosity. *Dip into the beer, old sport.* Pale ale in dozen-packs, great tower beside the desk. Drank four to my one, the greedy sod. Give a hell of a lot for a few of those packs now! Never crossed my mind it might be the last real beer I was destined to drink – if canned pale ale deserves to be called real beer, which, by God, compared with *Moskovskoye* or *Zhigulyovskoye* it certainly does! Bar-bores here have a knack of folding the label to make *Zhigulyovskoye* to read *khuyovoye* – it's like folding *Bass* to read *Piss* – not that anyone ever would . . . God, if I'd known I'd have downed two to his one and stuck a few in my pocket!'

Reminded of Ben Gunn and his hankering for cheese, Ashweald offered to supply Lager – *Tuborg, Carlsberg* – from the *Beryozka*. Peter had only to say where to ship it.

Peter brightened at once. 'Here,' he cried, 'here! I'll show you where a key's hidden. This week some time, yes? Not next – too near when Kirill's due.'

'Tomorrow evening – perhaps even afternoon?'

'God, yes! I can't wait! I'll be standing at the door with my glass in my hand . . . Look, have some roubles for a taxi. We're a wee way off the Vyborg Highway, continuation of Primorsky Prospekt where I picked you up. You can study the route when I drive you back. Got enough sterling for beer?'

'They take credit cards.'

'In which case, get a tidy load while you're about it. Knock it off the price of the picture. I'll have to cache it somewhere, but I'll think of something.'

'You must tell me what you want for the picture.'

'What will you give?'

'I'd rather *you* named a price.'

'It's my best,' he said, as if thinking aloud. 'My best.' Then, with sudden decision, 'Shall we say a thousand?'

'A thousand,' Ashweald confirmed extending a hand which Peter, perhaps from surprise, was slow to take.

'We did say sterling?'

'No, but we will.'

'Take a bit of smuggling in, that amount of cash.'

'Simpler for me to open a credit-card account for you to draw on.'

'Simpler in theory, perhaps, but not, in practice, for me . . .'

At about midnight they came in from the balcony. Peter switched on table lamps in various parts of the room, produced more vodka, and stretched himself, like Ashweald, on one of the several ottomans. 'Come in May or June,' he said, addressing the ceiling as if at the dentist's, 'and you shall have your painting. Or leave it till August and do a repeat of the course. I'll give you a phone number. Keep it in your head. Don't write it down anywhere. Just say *Can't manage this evening*. Or if I don't answer say *Tell Pyotr Petrovich, Kolya can't manage this evening*, and ring off. In Russian of course. Then be at the temple at nine on the next day . . . Remember all that?'

Speaking with the exaggerated care he employed when driving home from a pub, Ashweald said he would. His eyes were taking longer to reopen after each blink. No, he mustn't waste time in sleep, he must, must keep awake . . . He swung his feet to the ground, took breath and managed to say without slurring, 'What about the trial – tell me about it.'

'There wasn't much of one. Never is when you plead guilty. Bit like a headmaster's bollocking . . . Bags of self-righteousness. *I have listened, listened attentively, to all that your counsel has urged on your behalf –* '

' – Which was *in camera*.'

'More's the pity. Quive-Rivers was good. Very good. *I've listened attentively*, says the judge, licking his thin lips like a client moving off with a whore. *Far too much of this traitorous conduct going about*, he says, bringing the thing down to the level of food poisoning or 'flu. *And so to punish you, deter others and safeguard this country's security, there must be a very heavy sentence* . . . More lip-licking. *Fourteen years is the maximum that I can award* . . . Thank God for that, I thought, seeing the nasty gleam in his eye. *Fourteen years* he repeats, savouring it, *and that is what I propose to award – on each of the four charges, four terms of fourteen years to run consecutively, to make a total of fifty-six years in all* . . . '

Dropping the judge's voice he reverted to his own. 'I couldn't believe it. Couldn't take it in. The silence was what impressed itself on me most at that moment – utter silence, total absence of sound, movement, even breathing . . . Like you hear after a really outstanding performance – half a dozen times in a lifetime, if you're lucky, when thoughts and emotions are so engaged that they go rolling on after the music finishes. My judge wasn't that kind of performer, but the silence was that kind of silence. It was broken by Veronica's fainting and falling. Then I saw my mistake. I should have pleaded not guilty, brought a jury in on the act, put up a fight, not offered myself for slaughter.'

'What line did Quive-Rivers take?'

'Dirty-game nature of espionage, and therefore we should react with understanding rather than shock or surprise when one of our players becomes infected. On the other hand, where a man secretly changes allegiance in what is, essentially, a secret war, we may see it as an act of courage on that man's part if he elects to stay and fight in secret on that front where most damage is being done, in secret, to the country he now prefers. That this should be so is an occupational hazard that both sides should expect and accept. He said the same – only more forcibly – at the appeal, although at the appeal he threw in a point that had never occurred to me until then. A point so bloody near the knuckle it brought me up with a jolt. It would be wrong, he said, *to pass sentence with any intention of placating allies.* I'd forgotten till then that the Yanks put up most of the *Lucky Dip* capital. I don't think I even told the people here about that.

'It was sunny autumn weather when they took me to Parkhurst. You might have thought it was summer. I had a little grilled window to look out of. Sea like linoleum. Mist. Golden, apple-golden sun. Yachts, ferries sliding suddenly into view and just as suddenly out of view again. Fog horns. Gulls. I thought of Gwithian. Wondered if I'd live long enough to walk that beach again. And I felt low – lower than my lowest till then, which had been as a little boy, coming to after having my tonsils out and finding nobody there. I tried to hold my breath until I died – I felt so miserable with the pain and the loneliness – but then my parents came and the moment passed. This time it was Warburton who came. The screws passed my handcuff chain around some fixture and left us alone. No beer now. Just the stink. There must have been a bar on the ferry.

'*Bloody sorry, Pete*, that was the first thing he said. *Pete*, I ask you! No one ever called me that, even at school. *Bloody sorry Pete*, he said, *the old act seems to have come a bit unstuck . . . But not to worry. We'll spring you*, he said, *debt of honour. Serve a year or two, show willing* – those were the bastard's very words – *take it like a man* – Christ! – *and we'll see you right, get you to the Union, if that's where you want to go. That's a promise. I won't say shake* – glance at handcuffed hands. *But there's one bloody big condition. Once there, you keep your head down. You do not go public. You do not write any books. You do not give interviews. Whatever you hear or glean, you keep your head down*.

'God, the warmth, the golden sunlight of that crossing! Something you remember for ever – like those enjoyable cigarettes in the prefects' shrubbery . . . Volvo-loads of children, any number of cars with just one man and one woman in them . . . The sheer holiday atmosphere! Veronica and I could have been one of those couples, looking at the white prison-van, not seeing the bloody thing for what it was. But Veronica was back in the flat dying . . .

'The three years' solitary, they said, were because of all the live classified Intelligence still in my head. What cock! When I came out of solitary I shared with a chap called Jim Pearl. Sympathetic sort of bloke. Kept his pop turned down. Didn't mind me painting for hours in silence. Jim went out on parole over a period of months before his release, and that's when we started talking about my release, as he put it. Not a word about the Firm, or to connect him with it. But I couldn't see then, and I can't see now, why the hell he should have been willing to risk another stretch, for the dubious pleasure of getting me off mine. He was the man for the job all right. They couldn't have picked a better. There weren't many weak points in the system, but in his fifteen years he'd spotted all there were. He'd calculated down to the last second how to turn them to advantage, and when it came to doing it for real, he was superb. Outside, the arrangements were way out of Jim's league. They most definitely bore the stamp of Warburton.'

'What was so special?'

'Midget sub. Parent standing a long way out. I loathed every minute.'

'Russian?'

'Very. First time I had to speak it for real!'

*Vanishing Trick* told a different story – of hiding up on the island for a very long time, of changing appearances, of motoring, *à la Buchan*, to the Yugoslav border, where Peter had driven on alone to vanish for ever. But there seemed no point in dragging that in. Jim, who alone knew what part he had played, was long dead, victim, so continental journals had asserted, of a dose of radiation discreetly administered by one side or the other.

'All of which,' Peter concluded, 'is strictly between you, me and that bloody easel . . .'

Fired by vodka, sustained by sausage, they reminisced the night away, hopping from topic to topic as they'd done at Cambridge in the days when they'd had nothing much to reminisce about. At six, they hauled themselves to their feet, went out into the morning and walked by the water's edge. What little could be seen of the Gulf in the mist was still placid and without ripple. The crunch of their shoes in the coarsely-ground sand was for long the only sound. Then, near at hand in the resinous mist, a curlew called, and its familiar voice seemed to Ashweald as alien to that setting of carved balcony posts, ornate gable ends, oily sea, black firs and mushroom-white-barked birches, as the sound of English.

Using Kirill's mirror to shave, and for all he knew, Kirill's razor and brush, Ashweald wondered what would have happened if he had taken Kirill's notes back to the hostel with

151

him. Was it weakness, the gullibility of old age and the softening effect of the beauty of Leningrad that suggested to him that Kirill may well have had no sinister motive?

Peter took the earth track leading from the *dacha* through the firs to the highway, slowly, skirting humps and potholes with skill in the limited space available. 'Whenever I drive this bit,' he said, 'I think of that track over the towans which takes you to Gwithian beach.'

'That's been tarred over since your time. I don't think you'd care for it now.'

'By God I would not! When we were boys, that track was adventure! Every so often, your father or mine would take a car and trailer and us, to collect the driftwood we'd gathered off the beach . . . Up and down over the dunes, it was like being in a little boat. It was always autumn or winter. I can smell it, feel it – that grass-scented drizzle that never really soaks. I can hear the waves roaring like a gale in a forest. I can see the lighthouse, white against the slate-grey sky, brilliant white foam shattering against its rock. If I ever came back, I'd just sit and paint it, over and over again . . . It's a bloody great symphony that bay, hell to put on canvas, but worth every minute spent trying . . . Part, I suppose, of what attracts me here is that at heart it's as primitive as Cornwall. It's certainly as granite based. Do you often go back?'

'As often as I can. When the children were small, we used to rent a cottage off the lane to Portreath. When there were just the two of us, we used to put up at the inn.'

'Pendarves Arms. By the fork. Right for Hayle. Left for God knows where . . . Ah, it seems so near, and yet so far . . . Tell you what, if you go before your next trip here, will you make me a recording? Ninety minutes of waves – two whole sides of a cassette. Preferably with the tide coming in, from as close to Godrevy as you can get. Will you do that for me? Humour the nostalgia-racked expatriate?'

'I'll do it at half term, last week in October. Pity I can't post it on.'

'A pity, yes, but you can't. Still, that last week in October I'll be with you in thought. Pale summer it'll be . . . Nippy in the mornings, wisps of mist . . . You will do it? If it came to the choice, I'd rather have that recording than a thousand quid's worth of beer . . . '

They swung right onto the highway and joined the traffic heading for the city.

'What part did Archie play when the balloon went up?' Ashweald asked.

'Archie? Archie was in the States. I wished he hadn't been, though I can't see what difference he'd have made . . . Except that he's honest, which not many buggers in the Firm are. Dear old Archie! Shame I can't send him some greeting. Must be Head of Ops by now, well in the running for Director . . . '

'I don't think so. I heard somewhere that Head of Ops was Warburton.'

'Christ!' He pulled out and started passing a string of lorries which proved to be much longer than expected. An enormous coach came bearing down on them, horn blaring, headlights full on. It was a very near thing. 'Sorry about that. But the thought of them preferring Don to Archie – Christ, I ask you!'

'But Don, as I remember him, was no fool. He saw plenty to criticize, which isn't a bad sign.'

'In the pub he'd criticize, yes, all red-faced grin and dripping moustache. But that was just his way of sounding for reliability, tapping the old crate for signs of worm . . . Put me in mind of Hamlet's stepfather, Warburton did. Beware bar bonhomie, say I. Tends to be as fake as the horse-brasses! But this is it, Nick. Palace Square's at the end of yon wee street. Out quick when I stop. Don't forget the waves! Promise!'

He stood and watched Peter roar away and remembered how he had watched Sue drive away to her death – move off, more sensibly and steadily, down the drive on which their house stood, brake, pause, turn left into a clear road just as a madman, till then invisible, chose to exploit his 0-to-60 capacity to overtake on the bend. If only *he*, not Sue, had set out on that shopping trip . . . Sue, the honourable, the idealistic – his conscience, the impulse for such little good as he had done . . . Sue . . .

He shook his head as if to dispel the image of the crash. Of all that Peter had said in ten hours of talking, one phrase kept clamouring for attention. *Products were my pigeon, not cases* . . . The phrase, as it stood, was ambiguous, not in itself a proof that Peter did know about Komarov. That Komarov was, in Firm terminology, a *case*, not a *product*, was a conclusion Peter might easily have jumped to haphazard. Equally, it might have been an unguarded admission. Peter *had* read the book – his knowing that it said nothing about Veronica was proof of that. He *had* read the book, yet was concerned to deny knowledge of it, and particularly of the Komarov affair . . . Komarov must have seemed to offer the very break Peter had been hoping for, something spectacular . . .

He crossed from one side of Palace Square to the other, and walked a good stretch of Nevsky Prospekt, careless for the first and only time of the magnificence of both.

# 11.

Play a sort of secret Poirot, he'd been told in effect, and that's what he'd done, and here he was with a lot of undercover unearthings which he either could not or would not communicate further. Did he know himself what they added up to? Certainly not the solution of a mystery. But it might be in the nature of a real-life mystery to have no solution, a mystery being, essentially, only the visible portion of an iceberg and no good guide to the shape of the whole. The solution propounded to any real-life mystery must always owe a debt to delusion or illusion, but never so great a debt as when the real life involved is that special subdivision of those whose profession it is to deceive – those eternal conjurors caught, like grimacing urchins, by a change of wind, and condemned to remain as they are, contorted for ever.

The familiar buff-coloured *Zhiguli* went by as he entered the street of the hostel. Back in England he would see, waking one morning, that it was 4.10 a.m., and remember: he's at it now, this very minute, the little fat driver of the buff-coloured *Zhiguli* in his navy-blue suit – wiper-blades, wing-mirror . . . into the boot . . . then back to insert bits of rubber to keep the metal arms off the glass. All over Leningrad, perhaps all over the Soviet Union, people would be doing that. But there was the hostel cat seated on the step in the sun, regardant, front paws curving elegantly in and out like chairlegs. And there was Irina. He opened his arms and they ran together in an embrace.

'Oh, but you smell of garlic and Russian soap! Oh,

Nicholas, I was so worried. Carvel said you weren't back. Your bed hadn't been slept in.'

'The bridges were up, I couldn't get back. Had to sleep on a sofa.'

'You look as if you haven't slept at all. Come and have breakfast.'

Reflected in the window of the *gastronom*, where there was nothing whatsoever displayed, they might have been father and daughter, uncle and niece, grandfather and grand-daughter – in short, any combination other than a man and a woman teetering on the brink of God knew what – perhaps even of falling in love.

Carvel was at the *Visla* before them, and not in the best of moods. 'You must, simply must always leave an address or telephone number,' he insisted, receiving a repeat of Ashweald's sketchy explanation to Irina. 'Here in the Union anything is possible!'

'Next time I will, without fail,' Ashweald said.

'Missed a lively session last night. Set the joint jumping, didn't we Irina?'

She smiled bleakly.

'Could I, do you think, plead a consultation this after-noon?' Ashweald asked, changing the subject abruptly.

'Don't see why not. Have you actually got one?'

'Need to ring home. The place never seems to be open at the times when we're free.'

'No problem. I'm seeing his nibs before morning classes. And you, Irina, do you want one too?'

'No I do not. It's the Pushkin afternoon. I wouldn't miss that for anything.'

In the morning break they walked together outside the block.

'It wasn't actually a very nice party,' she said. 'Ernie and Eleanor got a singsong going with the younger contingent. After a while Carvel came round knocking up everyone who wasn't there, saying it was a golden opportunity to practise turns for the end-of-course party. Tatiana said yes, we'd love to, and it was quite civilized and jolly for a bit, then a lot of Yugoslavs and East Germans gate-crashed, bearing *slivovitz* and *Schnaps*. Eleanor hooked onto a great swarthy Montenegrin and danced like a teenager. I edged towards the door, meaning to escape through East Germany, as we did once, but I got dragged into the whirl. Eleanor called to me that I danced like a Russian. Do you think she knows?'

'I doubt it. But I'm sure she's somebody to be on your guard with. I certainly wouldn't, if she ever invites you, go visiting any of her local friends.'

'I thought you liked the ones you met.'

'I've had doubts since . . . '

'Tell me more, Nicholas, tell me more.'

'Just a feeling. It may be pure imagination, but they have a way of nudging you towards the illegal.'

'Offering to buy jeans – which you don't wear – or give you roubles for sterling?'

'That sort of thing, yes.'

'I washed my hair.'

'It looks very nice.'

'Oh, God, the bell. Tea at the *Astoriya*? You won't let me down?'

'Tea at the *Astoriya*. I'll wait in that little park opposite St Isaac's from five on. Don't worry if you're late. I'll have a book. I shall want to hear all about Pushkin's house.'

'I think you're up to something Nicholas. Something to do with last night . . . It can't be a ballerina, the ballet's on vacation . . . Hope it's not a fiery gypsy girl in a swirling saffron skirt, one of those who seem to haunt Gorky Gardens!'

'Who haunts Gorky Gardens?' Lady Tatiana asked with a twinkle as she hurried past. 'Phonetics. Double lesson. I'm going to be first at the Language Lab. Get the machine that works.'

157

When everyone had driven off in the coach to follow in Pushkin's footsteps, he engaged a taxi from the rank near Kazan Cathedral. Hearing that it was to be a beer-buying expedition and that he could count on a dozen for himself, the driver brightened. And throughout the tedious queueing at check-outs, while Finns, Americans and heaven knows who paid in currencies for which the assistants had no change, he attended Ashweald as zealously as any chauffeur his titled master in Bond or Jermyn Street. At last, with thirteen dozen loaded and the time just after three, Ashweald went to telephone. The driver promised to wait, and Ashweald was relieved to find the office empty. He filled out a form, the sad-faced assistant took the money due, and vanished to operate some concealed apparatus. He paced to and fro in the modernistic gloom, five minutes, ten, fearing all the time that his driver might be tempted to vanish with the one hundred and fifty-six cans of Lager. Suddenly a bell shrilled, the assistant lifted a receiver, listened, then announced that his call was connected to Kiosk No. 3.

'Margaret?'

'Daddy! How nice!'

'You're wonderfully clear. All right? And the animals?'

'Rob misses you. Keeps looking up the drive at the time you come home from school. Victoria left a dead squirrel in your study yesterday. The tortoises seem to know winter's coming. They've stopped eating.'

'And you, darling, are you really all right?'

'Perfectly. I've just cut the grass. Oh, and I've put more slug stuff by the lettuces – they're getting holes in them.'

'What are you doing?'

'Swotting Physics.'

'Don't overdo it.'

'I won't. I'm enjoying it actually. I'm going to see if I can't do really well, like Geoff.'

'No reason why you shouldn't. How is Geoff?'

'Still in Vienna with Käthe. He rang last night. He said

give you his love and he wishes he was there with you.'

'Give him and Käthe my love if he rings again.'

'Are you having a nice time?'

'Wonderful. Got my picture postcards yet?'

'Not yet. Don't suppose you've got my letters either?'

'Post takes about a fortnight, so don't write to me after today.'

'OK. Where are you phoning from?'

'Telegraph office on Nevsky Prospekt.'

'I've heard of that. Must be awfully exciting to be there.'

'It is. The Nevsky, I mean, not the telegraph office – that's a bit like a funeral parlour. Rob's all right, you say?'

'I can see him from the window, stretched out in the sun by the Christmas tree. I'm just going to pull a lettuce for lunch, and some radishes. Look after yourself, Daddy. Nice to hear you. Lots of love.'

He managed to say his own farewell before the line went dead. He could see Margaret pulling a paper tissue off the roll as she passed through the kitchen, for a nose blow. See her passing into the garden to comfort Rob. That was Daddy, she'd say, all the way from Leningrad, and he's all right. He's all right. She'd be kneeling, face against his head, arms about his powerful shoulders. Then she'd spring to her feet, pull the lettuce and the radishes and happily set about washing them.

It was gone! The taxi was gone! He stared in disbelief. He who had never in his life opened garage door or returned to parking place to find his car missing, now knew the feeling. His drink, not his car, had been stolen, but the reaction was the same: utter disbelief! He stood at the kerb where the car should have been, looked up and down, and then, also with disbelief, spotted the driver waving from the entrance to Gogol Street.

'Trouble with *ORUD*,' he explained.

'*ORUD*?'

'Traffic Police. I've parked in Gogol Street. I thought I'd

159

come and tell you, then I thought I'd better not leave the beer.'

The driver was not as proficient as Peter at avoiding potholes, and slowed almost to a halt so that the question he had been leading up to should be fully audible. 'Is it true,' he asked, 'really true – not just propaganda – that in the West most shops are full of goods, like the *Beryozki* we've been to, and that there's a choice of things – beers, wines, foods, clothes, cars?'

Concerned to avoid the we've-got-it-you-haven't line, Ashweald admitted that, broadly speaking, yes, it was.

The driver was shocked. 'Lord, how confusing! How can people ever know what to buy? With a car there might be as many as ten to choose from – if you include imported cars – is that not so?'

'More like a hundred,' Ashweald confessed. 'Maybe more.'

The driver stopped and rested his forehead on the wheel. 'Lord God, what a wasteful, chaotic kind of production! How does the West survive?'

Ashweald forebore to mention that whole publications were devoted to comparing cars, washing machines, toasters, any article you liked to name, with the aim of establishing the best value for money.

'And of those hundred cars, will all be readily obtainable? With ample sets of spares?' the driver persisted.

'Yes. But spares are never bought until there is a need for them.'

The driver eased the taxi forward. 'Such over-production and over-efficient distribution must surely involve as many drawbacks as under-production and poor distribution,' Ashweald heard before the din of the car reasserted itself.

Peter was not waiting at the door with his glass in his hand, and so Ashweald retrieved the key from its hiding place, and with the driver's help stacked the cartons of beer where Peter had shown him. He was more conscious now of the secret stirrings and creakings of the timber, more aware of the oppressive gloom of the fir forest. The sea, glittering dazzlingly, seemed to rival the sun in radiating and concentrating heat upon the *dacha*. Before leaving, he stole a quick look at his picture. Like the room, and the tray, bottles, glasses and coffee things, it had remained untouched, but its own serene life shone forth undiminished . . . A moment, rescued, rendered permanently secure from the weathering of time, the ravages of man . . .

He left his taxi in Ostrovsky Square. He offered a tip but the driver declined it, declaring himself sufficiently rewarded with the beer.

'Don't drink it while you're driving,' Ashweald warned. 'It's stronger than you'd expect.'

The driver saluted and swung away towards the Pushkin Theatre. As soon as he was out of sight, Ashweald entered the Saltykov-Shchedrin Library, showed his reader's card and mounted the fine staircase, struck by many points of similarity with the ascent to his Old-Firm office. In a little while he was sitting at the same table with the same pile of books as on his first visit. In the German translation of *Lone Battle* he turned to the page where Warburton's telegram was quoted and read and re-read the preamble:

$$= TOP\ SECRET = URGENT = DIRINT\ PERSONAL$$
$$= FROM\ 309 = PER\ XTX = BEGIN\ . . .$$

Allowing for the distortion of translation, something was still wrong with it, something which wasn't wrong with the rest of the signal. He must have noticed it subconsciously the first time he read it, stirring into life a tooth-like nerve which, on the drive back from the *dacha*, had started throbbing with an insistence that could not be ignored. He determined to sit there until he saw what it was – even at the cost of keeping Irina waiting.

161

He looked away from the page and considered his near neighbours, young and old, pretty and prim, shapely and rugged, scholarly and not so scholarly, all reading as if their lives depended on it, never for a moment raising their eyes. He thought back across the many years to the XTX-signals he himself had sent. There was a special pad of pink forms. Each page had distinctive boxes for preamble and text, the purpose of which was to facilitate encipherment. Seven preamble boxes, like the seven days of the week, a subject for jokes about Creation. Seven boxes: *Classification; Priority; Serial Number; Addressee; Sender; Method of Transmission; Date and Time of Origin* . . .

= *TOP SECRET* = *URGENT* = *DIRINT PERSONAL* = *FROM 309* = *PER XTX* = *BEGIN.* . .

A five-part preamble for seven boxes! Missing were the serial number and the date and time of origin. Why were they missing? Why?

The wording of the text was typical, and to that extent, authentic – peculiarly so, considering the unreality of most of the stuff concerned with the Firm and its workings. *Given*, then, the text of an authentic signal, *required to prove* was the connection between it and certain events. *Method*: let the mind, computer-fashion, sift the ideas that suggest themselves computer-fashion.

He tried first to visualize the pink form, then to fill in the boxes as they came. Yes, yes, of course! The serial number would be printed in its box already, like the *PER XTX*! So the serial number had either got lost in the process of translating and editing, or else was not there for the simple reason that it had not been on the actual signal form. An author with access to an actual signal form would have to be Firm, or a trusty acting for Firm. And he – or she – must have had access to an original, may well have reproduced an original exactly . . . He or she . . . Why should suddenly

162

the thought obtrude that Eleanor and Warburton would make a bloody good pair, be a godsend to the turnover of any bar . . . ? But he was becoming fanciful. He must concentrate, concentrate . . .

An XTX-signal, on the face of it complete and genuine, except for serial number and time and date of origin . . . He stared unseeingly at the page considering the possibilities generated by his mind, as once he had considered variations of openings at chess, postulating simultaneously an older, more venerable Warburton than *his* Warburton, an infinitely more powerful and, to him, unpredictable Warburton, standing in Vienna with that signal in his hand . . . An ambitious Warburton.

An XTX-signal, perhaps with the printed serial number obliterated – in which case it would be dead and unsendable because uncipherable – or perhaps a photostat of a photostat of the signal sheet, so that the liquid-paper obliteration on the first photostat should not be detectable. Why? For security? A great deal turned on the serial number of a signal. But why should the date and time of origin also be obliterated or omitted, leaving so much date evidence in the body of the text?

'I'm sorry – have you an india-rubber? I've dropped mine and can't find it.' The whisper came from his companion at the table, a girl with raven black hair like Irina's.

'Of course.' He felt in his pockets. Healthy, intelligent, attractive, terribly serious, she waited expectantly. 'Please keep it,' he said, handing over British public school property and returning his eyes to the page.

Suppose Tommy Dawson to be the 861 of the XTX-signal. Tommy had got starred Firsts at Cambridge against Ashweald's unstarred. Tommy would have done well at the ice-breaking stage and in the opening moves, but thereafter, against Komarov, would have been British school champion v. Soviet Grandmaster. Komarov might have founded a combination on an early pawn sacrifice, Peter being that pawn . . . *Yes, I will act as your agent. I can tell you of someone on your side who is working for ours – how's that for a start?* Peter, usefulness outlived, practically on a plate with pepper, salt, mustard and trimmings . . . Possible. But unlikely. Anyone as well placed as Peter would be an invaluable long-term investment. No matter how long he stayed bogged down in *Lucky Dip*, he would pass to other things eventually. They wouldn't ditch Peter, unless they'd someone better placed. So much for that possibility . . .

Warburton. Warburton and his ambition. A factor which Komarov, for all his brilliance, might not have built into his calculations, might not have allowed a margin of safety for. Warburton, knowing little, but obsessed with an image of Warburton serving up a Soviet ambassador to his masters and being, in due course, rewarded with a knighthood. To hell with running Komarov as an agent, he'd think, to hell with running and organizing that . . . Get him over, put him in the bag, force him to come if need be . . . *Here, Tommy, is a photostat of the signal that goes to London if Komarov's not with us by 2000 on 14th. Let him study it. He'll see the score. If, as he hints, they've got a man in the Firm, Komarov will see this as a sentence of death . . .*

What if the signal then got sent by accident, prematurely . . . Just Warburton's mark to bung the pink form automatically into his action-tray before trotting off to Tommy with the photostat. The original would have a serial number. The omission of date and time of origin would not necessarily be queried by a cipher clerk, especially in view of the *Urgent* priority.

Hypothesis. All hypothesis.

Fourteen years for Komarov, fourteen years for his wife, fourteen years for Tommy Dawson, fourteen years for *Lucky Dip*, totalling, perhaps too conveniently, fifty-six years . . .

Hypothesis. All hypothesis.

The spiriting away of Irina – had that been for her own good, or for the good of the Firm? Could it be that some

164

Kipling enthusiast in the Firm had seen Irina as a modern Kim? Hell! It was after five! Irina would be waiting! He delivered up the books, shot out into Ostrovsky Square and took a taxi to the *Astoriya*, finding the reckless, high-speed driving overcautious and slow.

But Irina was not waiting. Disappointed, he sat down on one of the seats in the sun. He looked up at the dome of St Isaac's, gleaming warm and secure against all ills beneath its 100 kilograms of gold – the figure was a guide's – a monstrous piece of dentistry. Of the twenty-four angels perched on the balustrade surmounting the drum of the dome he could see exactly twelve. He considered the squat minarets of the unbelled bell-towers under their golden cupolas, the strutting pigeons, the statues, the Old Church Slavonic inscription above the portico facing him: *My house shall be called a house of prayer* . . . How many who read that were aware of the continuation . . . *but you make it a den of robbers*?

'Nicholas.'

Lowering his gaze he saw Helen Blore, plain but unmistakably sultry, in a crisp print frock. She sat down beside him exhaling a subtle perfume, and opened her handbag.

'Note from Irina.'

In her clear pleasant hand, Irina had written in Russian:

*My dear Nicholas,*

*Something's cropped up to prevent my keeping our date. Explanations later – nothing to worry about. Do have tea as usual yourself – I shall think of you sitting at our table and you mustn't disappoint me. Don't wait up. I'll be late. I press your hand, eternally your Irina.*

The whole tenor of the note suggested Repino and filled him with unease.

'Not bad news?' Helen was looking at him curiously.

'No. Thank you for bringing it. How was the Pushkin tour?'

'As always. Pushkin, for me, lives in his works. Where he lived, where he sat, where he slept, where he read, where he thought, where he wrote, where he fought, where he died – those places now are just – places. They're not Pushkin, never have been. But we still go on the same old Pushkin trail.'

He had thought of her as empty-headed. A longer listen to the microphone in Carvel's bedroom might have told him his mistake earlier.

'Did Irina enjoy it?'

'I don't know. I only saw her to speak to when she gave me the note.'

'When was that?'

'We were just leaving the Pushkin house on the Moyka and going on to the scene of the duel. She said she wasn't coming, she was going to slip off. She knew I was coming to the *Astoriya* afterwards because I'd said at lunch that today was salmon-caviar day and I wanted some . . . '

'Where was she slipping off to? Did she say?'

'No.'

Carvel being otherwise engaged, they had tea together. The talk was of Pushkin, and Helen talked interestingly, but Ashweald wished all the time that she was Irina. They walked from the *Astoriya* together by way of the Nevsky, which was not normally the way he went with Irina. As they passed the entrance to the Stroganov courtyard Helen took his arm and led him in. 'You'd never think there was such a haven of peace slap bang on the Nevsky,' she said. He agreed, and to his discomfort they tarried, looking in at the statues, as if at zoo animals.

'If you're missing Irina as much as I'm missing Tom, we could go and dance somewhere,' Helen suggested apropos of nothing.

'I'm afraid I don't dance.'

'What the hell! Only a means to an end. We could begin with the end . . . ' She said it with a laugh, but her eyes were intense and serious.

'Oughtn't we to wait patiently – you for Tom, me for Irina?'

'Being patient is so dull. A Leningrad evening's the time for romance.'

'You're a naughty girl.'

She turned down her lower lip, looking sultrier than ever. 'Yes, I am.'

Now was the moment for Ernie to come waddling, or Eleanor tripping, through the gateway to the rescue, but neither of them did.

'Come on, let's go back to the hostel and see if Tom's there,' he suggested desperately.

'So long as you've got something to drink in case he isn't.'

'Lukewarm Lager.'

'Lovely. I can do great things on that.'

Carvel, as good luck would have it, was there. Ashweald handed Helen over and slipped away to his room. His sleepless night was catching up on him. He swallowed half a tooth-mug of vodka to buck himself up, poured a few fingers more, and lay on his bed. What a waste to be lying exhausted in this loveliest of cities on the balmiest of evenings. What an incredible girl Helen was! One more minute, then he would get up, check his mikes, take a stroll by the water . . .

He was woken at last by cramp. He massaged his leg vigorously, and as the pain eased looked at the clock. Half-past seven. But no longer evening! He had slept for over twelve hours, not set the alarm, and missed Irina! He rushed to the bathroom for water, put the water to heat, but dressed so rapidly that it was only lukewarm when he took it to shave with. He determined not to cut himself, but did, badly. Ten minutes of dabbing were needed to stem the welling blood, and the minutes seemed like days.

The *Visla* was more densely packed than he had ever seen it. No one from the course was there.

167

He drank his coffee and ate his dry slice of bread looking at Irina's old home and at the window on the third floor that had been hers. The yellow wall was as bright, warm and inviting in the glaring sun as a freshly-plucked, freshly-sliced peach. From there she would have looked out into the sun when she woke, and this window, his window, would have looked black and chill like the rest of the shadowed embankment. From up there, bright bank and dark bank would meet and sway together on the water.

The women with the cement and hods of brick were making progress. Others were plastering, and yet others were applying the peach-yellow finishing. He crossed the road, keeping a wary eye open for charging cars, and just outside the *gastronom* bumped into Carvel.

'You're late from the *Visla*, I'm early for the Institute,' Carvel said. 'Conference with Chichibayev.'

'See Irina at breakfast?'

'No. Missed you both.'

On the stairs he encountered Lady Tatiana.

'Did Irina oversleep?'

'I'm sure not. I called out before I left but she didn't answer. I assumed she'd gone straight to the Institute.'

'She did come back last night?'

'Oh, yes. I was very late myself, but the key was up so she must have been back. Her light was out so I didn't disturb her.'

'Would you mind if I took your key now to make quite sure she's not overslept?'

'No, take it.'

As Lady Tatiana swung herself slowly down the remaining stairs, he raced up to their floor. Eleanor, whom he passed in the corridor, remarked that he was going the wrong way. Helen looked up from locking her door to blow him a kiss.

He unlocked the outer door, knocked at Irina's door, then

opened it. Irina was in bed. It was Irina and yet it was not. The colour of her face was much altered. He reached out a hand to touch her forehead, smooth the hair back from it, but before even feeling the stony coldness, he knew that she was dead, peacefully dead, the quilt straight and tidy, the sheet neatly and evenly turned over the quilt at the top. He crossed himself, went down on his knees beside the bed, lowered his face into the quilt. *Mir prakhu tvoyemu*, rest in peace, were the only words he could think of, and he said them over and over again. After a little while, he rose to his feet, looked for a mirror on the dressing table, and finding none, fetched Tatiana's. It was no good. No suspicion of breath came from Irina's lips. Hot tears dimmed his eyes, and for a while he gave way to them. 'Irina, Irina!'

He brushed away his tears, and when he could see clearly took stock of the room. There were no clothes, no personal effects about, but there were the two cases he had carried at the airport. He clicked one open, and saw the obvious. She had packed to save others trouble. The waste-paper basket was empty, but in the refuse bag in the entrance hall he found an empty vodka bottle and a small brown plastic container with a chemist's label *The sleeping tablets, one to be taken before retiring*, also empty. The glass from which she must have drunk the vodka to wash down the barbiturates was inverted on the bath to drain. He found no note. Her handbag, stood beside the cases, contained only money, personal documents and her wristwatch.

As well as grief, as well as shock, Ashweald felt through an icy, numbing incredulity a sense of hurt that grew more acute with each minute spent searching vainly for some message, some explanation . . .

He gave up looking at last and let himself into Tatiana's room. Here he replaced the mirror, and casting around with the inhibited movements of a walker in space, he found a square of card and a tin of charcoal sticks. With the charcoal he wrote a *do-not-disturb* notice boldly in Russian, and pinned the card to Irina's door. After which he stood for perhaps five minutes by her body, before kissing the cold forehead and going to find Carvel.

# 12.

They walked in the quadrangle where he had walked with Irina the day before.

'Why did she do it, Nick?' Carvel asked. He meant to sound incredulous and sympathetic, but an imbalance lent a slight harshness to his voice.

'I don't know.'

'Was she unhappy?'

'She didn't seem so.'

'Did you quarrel?'

'Ours wasn't that sort of relationship. There was nothing to quarrel about.'

'I'm sorry. I'm just being heavy footed, Nick. I don't really know where to start.'

'I suppose the first thing to do is inform Chichibayev. After that, ring our embassy. They will have to inform the next of kin and make arrangements about the body.'

'There'll have to be a post mortem, won't there?'

'I'm sure there will. But whether here or at home is something that will have to be decided.'

'We'd better go to Chichibayev together.'

Two battered mustard-yellow *Pobedas*, stencilled with the word *militsiya*, stood at the kerb by the hostel door. At the reception counter half a dozen men were standing, joking with the *dezhurnaya*. One was in civilian clothes, the others were in uniform. As Carvel and Ashweald entered, a stocky, grey-haired, kindly-faced man stepped forward and intro-

171

duced himself as Colonel Ponomarenko of Special Investigations. He had with him a surgeon, technical assistants and an official from the procuracy. He would like, he said, to inspect the body, take a preliminary statement, then perhaps remove the body to the mortuary, pending the arrival of representatives from the British Embassy. Did that meet with *gospodin* Carvel's agreement? If not, he would seal the room and take no further steps until the arrival of the embassy party.

'What do you think?' Carvel asked Ashweald in English.

'I don't think the body should remain where it is in this heat.'

'I agree.'

'And I agree also,' said Colonel Ponomarenko unexpectedly in excellent English. 'So shall we go ahead, gentlemen?'

'Let's go ahead,' confirmed Carvel, turning towards the stairs.

Colonel Ponomarenko and his colleague from the procuracy showed themselves to be courteous and efficient. Later that day a young Russian-speaking Second Secretary arrived by air, accompanied by the embassy doctor, and after viewing the body agreed to arrange transport to Britain for post-mortem examination. An inquest would then be opened, and probably adjourned until the return of the British party at the end of the course.

For the rest of the day Ashweald was taken many times, in English and Russian, over his discovery of the body and subsequent actions, and subjected to many near and distant relatives of the questions it had first occurred to Carvel to ask. And all the time he stonewalled as he had stonewalled to Carvel, but out of loyalty to whom – Irina or Archie – he hardly knew himself. Irina's late arrival, and from Italy, not Britain, paying her own fare, and the uncertainty surrounding home address, next-of-kin, and even place of work, were matters he left the Second Secretary to discover for himself. And when he did, Ashweald expressed himself no less mystified than the Second Secretary, and

172

sympathized that he should find it so hard to put the agreed arrangements in hand, and for reasons other than obstructive tactics on the part of the Russians. Indeed, in the face of their extreme helpfulness it was downright embarrassing to appear so badly at sixes and sevens. But at last there was a lull to it all, a lull that extended into final silence. The Second Secretary followed the doctor back to Moscow. Colonel Ponomarenko and his nameless colleague no longer came rattling to the door in their battered *Pobeda*, and life returned to normal.

And Ernie, who had once vowed he would save Ashweald's life, did more towards doing so in these days than he realized, by providing quiet, considerate companionship. *She were a great lass, Nick,* was his only comment, and thereafter he trotted along or effaced himself with the same unerring instinct as Ashweald's Labrador, for which Ashweald was eternally grateful.

On the day that the body was driven to Pulkovo in a tall ungainly khaki van without windows, Ashweald, Carvel, Lady Tatiana, Eleanor, Ernie and others followed behind in taxis. Colonel Ponomarenko awaited them at the airport building. The doors of the plain van opened to reveal six militiamen who slid the coffin out and shouldered it expertly. Lady Tatiana placed on the coffin the pink gladioli they had brought. Then, led by the colonel, the mourning party followed the bearers across the tarmac towards a blue and white *Aeroflot* aircraft. They saw the coffin taken into the luggage hold. The colonel saluted. At last they walked slowly back to the airport building and through it to the car park where their taxis were waiting. Carvel and Eleanor accepted a lift from the colonel, leaving Ashweald to escort Lady Tatiana.

'I'm glad of a chance to speak to you alone,' she said as soon as the taxi was under way. 'I never think one can really talk safely in those rooms at the hostel. People say they can pull a switch or something and hear every word that's spoken, and I shouldn't be at all surprised. But what I want to say, Nikolay

Karlovich, is this. Ponomarenko and that little whipper-snapper secretary unpacked Irina's cases, laid everything out on bed, chairs and floor, then asked could I tell if anything was missing – clothing, trinkets, jewellery, books . . . I looked, but it took no artist's eye to spot the obvious. Dear Mishka and the sketch of you he sits beside were both gone. I didn't tell Ponomarenko that. The fewer complications the better. Also I thought that you might have taken them as keepsakes.' Her shrewd eyes looked steadily from under a slightly raised forehead. 'Did you, Nikolay Karlovich?'

'No, I didn't.'

'Were they there when you went in?'

'I really can't say.'

'Mishka meant so much to her.'

'I know.'

'The dear girl would never have packed so tidily and forgotten two things of such importance.'

'Have you looked in your room?' he suggested. 'She may have put them there.'

'That is certainly a possibility . . . My room is so *zagromozhdena vsyakimi veshchami* . . . '

'Cluttered . . . '

'Yes, cluttered. I wish this damned thing would go even faster . . . It's so vexing. I was always going to attempt his portrait. Bears are so difficult. That is why I kept putting it off. Mishka, you know, although she never saw it, was a great betrayer of her origins – I won't say more . . . You see, I, I can remember when he and his brothers came on sale here, in *Gostiny Dvor*, oh, thirty years ago . . . ' She looked away. They were nearly at the hostel. The driver was slowing for the right-hand turn after the little humpbacked bridge. Ashweald patted the mottled hand that rested on a handbag of Gladstone proportions, but said nothing.

While Lady Tatiana rummaged vaguely, he sat where he had sat for his portrait and looked at pensive Irina being spied on by the griffons. Now Tatiana was pulling out from under the bed a portfolio which she dumped next to Ashweald. It was held shut by tapes which she had difficulty in unfastening. As he rose to help, the knot gave and the folder opened to reveal the sought-after sketch. She motioned him not to speak, opened the envelope paper-clipped to the mount and began to read, her face wooden and inscrutable. For a long time she stood and stared, while Ashweald stood and stared and fought an urge to rush forward and read over her shoulder. At last, at long last, she sank wearily down on the bed, holding out the letter for him to take. Irina had written in Russian:

> *Dear, dear Tatiana Leonardovna,*
>     *Not ingratitude – that very least of all – prompts me to return this to you for safe-keeping, but fear lest it complicate what does not deserve to be complicated. Remember me kindly. Ever your Irina. 14 August 4.30 pm.*

On an envelope from his pocket he wrote the words *Tell Carvel?* She shook her head violently. 'That would undo her work. Go and look in your room . . . Let me know if you find anything . . . '

He searched his wardrobe, drawers, cupboard, taking everything out, turning everything over, feeling in pockets. Then he did the same thing all over again, after which he sat gloomily on his bed with his last half dozen Lagers martialled before him. He pulled the ring of one, half wishing it was a hand grenade. He poured, sipped. Marinaded blotting-paper! He poured it down the sink.

Had she nothing, nothing to say to him? Nothing? Letting go, he plummeted unresisting into sickly depths of self-pity. Then, angrily, he dashed the tears away and just as angrily fought his way back up again. Against the searing agony of her loss, against the courage with which she had gone to her death, how feeble to be indulging so petty a sense of hurt!

He threw the empty can into the bin, returned the

remaining cans to the cupboard, tidied up. What had to be faced was that nobody told the whole truth ever. Because there never was a whole truth to tell. And possibly the most significant moment of his stay in Leningrad had been that which he had chosen to see no significance in, that which he had let roll away and lie forgotten under some heavy piece in the lumber-room of the mind . . .

. . . *Walking and talking with my parents' killer . . . walking and talking* . . . He'd taken it as a rhyming invention of her own, an original usage . . . Not as literal truth!

What clearer, what more precise warning could there possibly be than simply *to keep a weather-eye open for a seafaring man with one leg!* But when he appears, One-Leg, parrot on shoulder, Jim is disarmed . . . Jim refuses to connect, lets the obvious stare him in the face, pass him by . . .

Why, why, in all his obsession with the Stroganov Palace yard, had he not until now thought back to that moment when Irina had come walking out of the archway with a man . . . With a man of whom he had seen only the back . . . With a man who could so easily have been Peter . . . Peter whom she would have known then as Lomashev . . . Who had driven her from Repino in his car . . . Parked it in its place in the courtyard . . . *Let me show you a favourite subject of mine. Strangely, I don't think I've ever seen it by moonlight* . . . How natural to leave the car and walk the few steps to the hostel . . . How natural not to wish to accompany Irina too close to the hostel . . .

A tap on the door. Damn, damn, damn!

The door opened. Ernie poked his head round. 'Few of us going to the Swedish Table at the *Pribaltiyskaya*, Nick. Coming?'

'Thanks, Ernie, but I think I'll stay and write a few cards.'

'Sure?'

'Thanks, Ernie, yes.'

'Look in for a night-cap about eleven if you feel like it.'

'Love to. Thanks.'

He gave them time to get clear before himself setting out. Just short of the Nevsky there are a couple of telephone kiosks. He joined the queue. When his turn came, he dialled the number Peter had given him. There was, as on the several occasions since Irina's death when he had rung, no reply. He dialled the Martovs. Again no reply, but as he was about to ring off, Kirill's mother answered.

Disguising his voice, he said, 'Forgive my troubling you, but is Kirill Antonovich there, or Klavdiya Pavlovna?'

'Who is speaking?'

'From the faculty. An official matter.'

'They are still away,' the old lady said in her crystal-clear Russian. 'In Moscow.'

'Is it known when they return?'

'At the end of the month.'

'This month?'

'This month, August, yes.'

'I thank you most dutifully.'

As he stood on the edge of the pavement, undecided which way to go, a car tooted. He looked across to the taxi parked below the columns of the cathedral in the sun, and recognizing the grinning face, walked over.

'Like the beer?'

'Nectar! Praise be to God I still have some left. I drink just a can a day. I still have six more days of enjoyment. My little son prizes the empties for building towers.'

'So you wouldn't say no to some more?'

The driver beamed. 'I would say a very ready yes.'

'It seems I made the delivery too late. It's a question of collecting it back. Could you drive me out there now?'

'With pleasure.'

In the slowly failing light of evening, the sepulchral gloom of the dense fir forest to right and left was beginning to encroach on the track, open as it was to the sky, and the menace of the process was worthy of Hopper.

The key was still in its hiding place. What would he see when he opened the door? A right fool he'd look if the beer was gone! But the beer wasn't gone. The cartons stood stacked as they had left them.

'Would you mind loading them, while I fetch something from inside?'

'No, of course not.'

Standing in the study he was assailed by an unreasoning dread that the driver might drive off leaving him to his fate. The house had a bad feel. A creaking, as of stealthy footsteps, a sickly odour of wood as in an undertaker's workshop. Was that the car's engine? No, no, no! Skidding at corners he raced for the door. No, his trusty driver was merely backing up closer.

'Take your time,' he called, seeing Ashweald. 'I'll walk down and smell the sea. Such an idyllic spot.'

He returned to the studio, heart pounding as it might high on Everest. He would not feel safe until he saw the driver down by the sea, and he kept a constant look-out until he did.

Meanwhile he wrapped his picture in old copies of *Pravda* which, clumsy-fingered, he secured with string. With the parcel under one arm, he was about to scuttle out when he caught sight of a painting that was so vividly real as to make him gasp. A dead mouse in an English-style mousetrap, oil on a thick, postcard-sized rectangle of wood, deeply varnished to create an illusion of glass. The sprung bar of the trap had descended as intended, breaking the fragile spinal column, killing the mouse within micro-seconds of its mouthful of cheese. Terrible, the greed, the pleasurable anticipation, the contented sense of accomplishment registered in every feature and in the tiny popping eyes. But more terrible the way in which, without the slightest distortion of mouse as mouse, those features were also suggestive of Peter's! Ashweald wrapped it in a single copy of *Pravda*, and slipped it into his hip pocket.

Rather than attract attention by carrying them into the

hostel, he made the driver a present of the gross of Lager, at which the driver refused payment and undertook to drive him free of charge for a long time to come – if not on this visit, then on his next. He wrote down his name and telephone number, and Ashweald felt that he had gained an ally and a friend.

Carvel, on his way to breakfast, was knocked down in Dzerzhinsky Street by a car that must have come over the bridge too fast for him to dodge. If first aid had arrived quicker, he might have survived. The distraught driver of the offending car and passers-by, Ashweald amongst them, did their best, but that best was inadequate. Carvel died in the ambulance. His last words were to Ashweald, and formed a request that he should, when in London, phone such-and-such a number and leave a message for *Sir Donald* that he would understand. The message was, simply, *Negative – no trace of subject*.

The British survivors, now thirteen in number, held a meeting in the common-room area of their corridor, at which the chair was taken by Lady Tatiana, as Deputy. After several minutes' silence in token of respect for their dead companions, they agreed that the course should not be abandoned but should continue with Lady Tatiana as Leader, and that Dean Chichibayev be duly informed of this, as also of their wish to be excused from offering any end-of-course entertainment. All present were unanimous in expressing gratitude to their Soviet hosts for their under-standing attitude. And they noted with appreciation Nicholas Ashweald's willingness to attend, in due course, to the packing of Carvel's effects.

After the meeting everyone stood round in awkward silence. Eleanor took a long swig from a silver flask from her handbag and offered it to Ernie who refused, patting his stomach. Helen began to move in Ashweald's direction, slowly but surely, only to be beaten by Lady Tatiana.

'Nikolay Karlovich, I'd be grateful for your support if you can spare the time. Dean Chichibayev's expecting us. We can walk over now . . . '

In the street and away from the hostel she said, 'About that picture . . . I've examined it. The canvas can easily be removed from the frame and rolled. Shall I do it?'

'Would you?'

'It's a tragedy it's not finished.'

Ashweald said nothing.

'You'd better let me take it in my baggage. It won't look amiss. I'll say it's my work. My goodness, I wish it was!'

'Can you keep it out of sight until then? From Eleanor, above all . . . '

'Yes, of course.' She might have been agreeing to keep a birthday present hidden. 'Then perhaps one day in England you'll come and have a cup of tea and tell me, strictly between ourselves, who painted it. I'm intrigued. It's a Russian apprehension of a certain style of Impressionism. But no Russian would use a birch-tree quite so obviously . . . '

After their interview with Chichibayev, he left Lady Tatiana at the door of the hostel, and walked to the Stroganov Palace. Amongst the cars parked was a red *Zhiguli*. The registration number was Peter's. The ignition key was in place. No one had stolen the wipers.

Classes, lectures, films, expeditions, conducted tours – he took part in them all, and was glad of the way they ate into the day. In free time, after resisting the attentions of Eleanor and Helen as gently as he could, he avoided the company of everyone except Lady Tatiana, and occasionally Ernie. With Lady Tatiana he marvelled at the Impressionists in the State Hermitage. With Ernie he toured the Museum of the History of Leningrad, patiently explaining the texts to the exhibits. Alone, he sat for hours in the Summer Garden, and in the cool of the evening walked by the Moyka, the Griboyedov

180

Canal and the Fontanka, keeping close to the railings, his eyes on the water. His face wore a look which his children would have recognized – the look he wore when, hearing the mail-van turning, he strode across the lawn to fetch whatever it was, although he said he was expecting nothing. Each day too, he checked to see whether Peter's car was still standing in the courtyard, and found it was, its peculiar shade of red a jarring splash against the sober pale green of the palace and the exuberant green of the foliage.

Blue Bridge, which is as wide as St Isaac's Square, serves the Moyka more as a tunnel than as a bridge – a tunnel concealing a good hundred metres of river. The up-stream side of the bridge is the more agreeable: a row of limes runs from just opposite the *Astoriya* to the very edge of the Moyka, softening the effect of granite and railings. On the down-stream side, the eye is drawn to the austere Leningrad Municipal Soviet of Peoples Deputies, and there is no greenery to relieve the severity of stone and metal.

Walking up-stream along the Moyka Embankment towards nine o'clock on the evening of the 27th of August, eyes fixed on the water, Ashweald saw something well under the arch of Blue Bridge. The water was inky black, the light at that point poor, but as he stared, the something became unmistakable. It was a puffed-up area of red-and-white check shirt, swaying gently like a buoy . . . a shirt like that which Peter had been wearing when he had last seen him, a fortnight before, driving away in the red *Zhiguli*.

As everywhere, the railings were low, the sides were of smooth, vertical granite, and the water was deep. A non-swimmer, pitched in from the middle of the bridge from, say, the *Astoriya* end, would never even make the side . . . Swiftly and cleanly pitched in by abuse of a judo throw . . . Or simply overbalanced backwards . . .

Ashweald turned away. That was a corpse best left for others to discover.

Next day, after morning classes, they exchanged souvenir gifts with their Russian hosts, toasted each other in Russian champagne, took leave of their teachers, and retired to their rooms and the dreary anti-climax of packing. For a long while Ashweald tinkered with Carvel's cassette recorder, trying to discover the trick that would play back the track with the microphone transmissions. His hope was not to unearth some further secret, but to hear Irina's voice. And only after trying every possible combination of twisting, pressing, pulling and sliding did he admit himself beaten and shove the thing into one of Carvel's cases. Then he sat in his room and wondered what the hell he had done with his grip. He could see his case, but his grip was not inside it, he knew. Nevertheless he fetched it down and looked. No. Surely no one had pinched his grip – it was in an awful state. He passed a hand under his bed. Nothing. He took his torch, lay prone and shone it under. Ah, there it was. Thank God for that. Without it he'd be dished for carrying all the books he'd bought. He pulled it out, unzipped it – and there was Mishka staring unblinkingly up . . . Mishka and an envelope like the one left for Tatiana . . .

Mishka, in the manner of his kind, wore the distant, mildly amused facial expression of one unaffected by the affairs of men. Bears were like cats, *of* the house but aloof, and like cats, appealed especially to women . . . Nestling his cheek against the bear's face, he seemed to catch a scent – the scent of Irina's hair. 'Oh, Irina!' he exclaimed aloud. 'Irina, Irina!'

How theatrical, useless, empty! No – not entirely empty. Anguish was in the cry, anguish at the needless waste of life, of lives. Leaves stripped from the branch, flung on the heap, long before their proper autumn. Lives thrown away in the service of a game having relevance to nothing of human value. An evil, perverted, self-indulgent game! And in that cry too, was the anguish of discovering, concentrated in sense of loss, the irony of having loved without having conveyed to the loved one any sense of security.

He opened the envelope with a knife and slipped it, the letter still inside, between the pages of a book. Mishka he returned gently to the grip, and the grip to its place beneath the bed. After which, taking the book, he went out, locking the door behind him. Now in the corridor, on the stairs, in the street, he felt Irina's presence more strongly than at any other time since her death.

The seat in the Summer Garden where they had first sat together was empty. He quickened his pace, as if fearful that some rival might materialize out of thin air. His hand trembled as he drew out the letter, unfolded it and read, very slowly because of the trembling, hearing Irina's voice as if she were beside him, youthful, warm, alive . . .

> *I love you, Nicholas, more than anyone I have known, and wish – after all that you have done for me, after all that you yourself have suffered – that I did not have to cause you pain.*
>
> *I have always told you the truth, but I have, as you must suspect, held some things back.*
>
> *What I said when we were at* Mon Plaisir, *about the Little Mermaid, is what I can't overcome. It's too strong. It's no good now even trying to find my way back to life, which means you, along the dark path that it is given to me to follow.*
>
> *Don't grieve, dear Nicholas. Pray that our two countries may come together though we cannot. Look after Mishka. I will be with you both, if I can. Irina. 14 August 4.45 pm.*

In that beautiful garden in that most beautiful of cities on that finest of days, people were sunning themselves, healthy happy children were walking, holding tight to mother's or father's hand. One small girl, oblivious of the burning sun, dark pigtails flying, face intensely concentrated, was chasing a little red hoop in and out of the walkers. A little way off, another British tourist, white sun hat tilted over his eyes, was smoking a pipe, while his wife knitted, watching the passers by.